die

lady

die

To Jeff:
Hope you enjoy it!
Friends
Luis.

Die, Lady, Die

Alejandro López

with an afterword by Daniel Link

translated from the Spanish by Jay Miskowiec
translation edited by Luis Lemoins

ALIFORM PUBLISHING
is part of the Aliform Group
117 Warwick Street SE, Minneapolis, MN USA 55414
information@aliformgroup.com   www.aliformgroup.com

First published in Argentina by
Adriana Hidalgo editora, 2001

First published in the United States of America by
Aliform Publishing, 2005
English translation copyright © Aliform Publishing, 2005

Library of Congress Control Number 2004116968

ISBN 0-9707652-6-6

Printed in the United States of America
Set in Times New Roman

Cover art by Pat Badani, "El objeto de tu deseo"
Photo of cover art by Petronella Ytsma
Cover design by Caroline Fox

Contents

Die, Lady, Die   3

"Mass Media Totalitarianism:
Hope Over All"
an afterword by Daniel Link   139

Translator's Acknowledgments   145

1

ESCAPING FROM TOWN was a bloody nightmare. Three hours hidden in the bus station restroom, half the time shut up in a stall with the wooden door an inch from my nose and a crack to look through I could barely reach standing on tip-toe. From there I monitored perfectly all outside movement. Alert, with the five fingers of my right hand pushing against the filthy wood and stability hanging by a thread.

Every couple minutes images of Benito, my dead sister and mama passed through my mind, flickering like lights on a Christmas tree, lighting up one after the other and disappearing all at the same time. I was scared I'd been turned in and the station was full of cops in uniform showing around my photo or asking about my whereabouts. Terrified of never being able to leave Gualeguaychú and ending up in jail, surrounded by brawny women and mattresses stinking like piss, that same unbearable stench of the bus station restroom. Luckily I had the bottle of Anais-Anais perfume I managed to rescue when I escaped, and so the stay in that shitty stall wasn't quite so intolerable.

After an hour and a half I couldn't take it any longer. My legs hurt from standing on my toes and I think the perfume had released in me a general feeling of nausea.

I poked my head out, walked straight ahead, and fell weightlessly into a rickety old chair miraculously found next to the sink in the midst of that inferno. I didn't want anybody to notice how nervous I was, but the world was falling apart around me.

When I could finally focus and looked at myself in the mirror, I almost died of humiliation. Having cried all afternoon, I seemed as deformed as if I'd just come out of surgery. I applied the new Tsu foundation, but I couldn't perform a miracle, so I changed my t-shirt, put on my sunglasses and sat there still like the bathroom attendant, with my image completely changed and the enormous mirror before me that did nothing more than bring me back to reality.

It's true that I looked older than eighteen with the tone of that foundation, but even so I still felt like someone else. Though I was carrying the black leather backpack I've had since forever, I looked different to myself, as if my muscles had relocated to new places. Surer and stronger than ever, I thought nobody could stop me. Not even my mother.

Little baggage. I didn't want any memories of my previous life. What I did pack, though, was a totally killer black mini-skirt, a pair of slacks, three t-shirts that made me look skinny and some dirty panties I found at the last minute. Nothing else interested me. I had to keep space for my favorite things: the autographs of Menudo I had jealously guarded since age seven, my two photo albums of Ricky Martin, and a glass bottle of Villavicencio mineral water which he had personally given me at the discothèque Gualeguaychú-Pamela. A double-sized poster from *TV Guide* showing his whole leg where he looked naked, my medal of Our Lady of Lourdes, and the white handkerchief with an "E" embroidered in one corner and Ricky's sweat deeply impregnated in the cloth. That and Nélida Doménico's phone number were all I needed.

In another fifteen minutes the bus that would forever free me from Gualeguaychú was leaving. I'd become a robot and every two minutes I checked to make sure all the information on my ticket was correct: "Departure: 10 p.m. Destination: Buenos Aires. Seat: 13. Window. $15." And I put it back in the backpack, repeating the information under my breath to pass the time. I felt uncomfortable, observed, I needed to move my hands, and from taking it out and putting it back so much the ticket had become all torn, like my fingernails after such a day.

I felt like I was getting dehydrated. I'd lost gallons crying and I couldn't stop peeing, holding my nose and pushing with my legs, trying to keep my balance so I wouldn't touch the toilet seat.

Exhausted. Then Titina, the sales clerk at the record store Chorus, came skipping in like the apparition of some rabbit. Fake as ever and with the longest gaudiest fingernails that matched her sweater.

"Esperanza, what are you doing here?" she asked surprised in her nasal twang, almost peeing in her pants.

"I'm going to Buenos Aires," I confessed, "to have Ricky Martin's baby," and the second I said it I was sorry.

"But sweetie, he lives in Miami," she shouted through the open door of the stall, her panties at half-mast and her face contorted from the stench of piss.

"I know, but in October he's going to give a mega concert on 9 de Julio Avenue and I'm going to wait for him," I answered, "and since we've already agreed, I'm going to kill some time in Buenos Aires." She was holding her butt up and back, her hands pressed against her thighs, effortlessly keeping her back straight and ten inches off the toilet. Divine.

So she said to me, "Fine, when you see him send me a picture," all the while wiping her *cholila*, looking sidewise as if she were talking to some crazy person. Then, with a serious look on her face, she asked me, "Are you okay?" and I thought I was going to fall apart, and though I felt some inner need to tell her everything, I put my sunglasses on my forehead, looked at her with daggers in my eyes and made a threat. "You never saw me, Titina. Never," I repeated, zipping two fingers across my mouth. To change the subject, she asked me about Gloria, but she didn't even listen to the answer, and after sniffing her fingers she said goodbye with her little hand in the air, pointing her lime green fingernails towards the floor like a castanet. She had to run off because she was just about to miss her bus, and she skipped off just like she'd entered.

The sole fact of mentioning Gloria made me think I wouldn't see her any more, and then I started crying again. I remembered the morning we met and she showed me Spencer, her guinea pig, or when she was sick and I used to read to her from *Stories for Veronica*. Or when she would sleep over and we'd drink soda straight from the bottle because it was the closet sensation to the shortness of breath and the uncertainty being around boys stirred in our bodies.

I hid behind my sunglasses to quietly cry and not have to lock myself inside a stall again. Mama's screams tumbled over my head and I remembered the scene for the millionth time. First Benito's face coming into my room. He was an absolute hunk with his hair tied back in a ponytail and wearing a tight black t-shirt that almost showed his bellybutton. Of all mama's boyfriends he was the strongest. In one hand he was holding a spoonful of caramel sauce and in the other a little mirror. I was immersed in *TV Guide*, sprawled on my bed seething with hatred over Madonna's schedule while filming *Evita*. She wasn't going to slow down a minute. "No wonder she's always so skinny," I thought; in the background you could hear mama's hair dryer. Insufferable.

Saturdays at siesta time she looked like a Martian, sitting in the living room with a plastic hairdryer over her head that looked like the helmet of a diving suit plugged into the wall, completely disconnected from the outside world. And Benito asks me, "You want some, bunny rabbit?" and he gives me a big smile and shows me the spoon and I'm dying because I'm on a diet and don't want to fall off it but this is too big a temptation. And then I gather strength from who knows where, put down the magazine and although I'm fat as a cow, I answer, "A little," and my mouth starts to water. It's been two weeks since I've had anything sweet and my whole body is craving, screaming out asking me for it. He comes over to a corner of the bed, signaling that from there mama can't see us, and we listen for her hair dryer like some kind of alarm. Benito lowers his zipper, puts a little bit of caramel on the tip of his dick, spreads it around with his finger like he's giving it a facial and asks me to go on, he stands straight up and although I'm pretty scared I go for it, because when Benito says something I do it and that's that; I give in, close my eyes and lose myself.

When I've eaten all the caramel, he takes what's left but this time smears his whole dick with it. Then he tilts

7

the little mirror so he can see me good and signals with his tongue for me to keep going and he tries to see everything from above. I look in the other direction because I hate to see myself in close-up; he touches his stomach, lifts his hand and bites it and I see my reflection in the spoon, really small, with my nose where the metal curves so I look like a pelican, my lips stretched out and my chin big and wide. Deformed, and at that moment I raise my eyes to find mama's head suddenly peering through the door, without the hairdryer, her hair standing straight up from the static.

It was like a bucket of ice-cold water. Benito still had a hard-on, but I didn't even have time to let go of it before mama was pulling my hair and thrashing me around the room. Real hell. My whole body hit the nightstand, I bounced off the dresser, and without wanting to threw an elbow into my wooden butterfly that ended up rolling across the floor. Mama wouldn't stop. She dragged me out to the hallway and forced me down the stairs on my knees step by step, all nine, while she pushed my head down so I couldn't lift it. I'm sure I suffered shock or something because after that everything gets confusing. I know very well what happened, and although it's all in my head it seems like a movie with a lot of quick cuts.

She'd never hit me so many times and pulling my hair she screamed at me, "You evil little bitch!" I couldn't react, squatting, praying in a low voice, "Our Father who art in Heaven," and her, "You evil little bitch!" and me, "hallowed be Thy name." And the hair dryer plugged in like background music.

After that mama, completely out of her mind, hit me in the face with her fist, then with the first flower vase she found. And I had to defend myself because I couldn't take the pain any longer and despite being in the most awkward position, I gave her a slap that left her face trembling. Without thinking I gave her another and another. Three in all.

She reacted immediately. She stopped screaming, put one hand on her forehead and the other on her chest, and stumbled backwards. I thought she was going to faint but no, she staggered into the kitchen for a glass of whiskey, and without saying a word locked herself in her room with two turns of the key.

I just managed to reach my own room, my mind a complete blank. No trace of Benito anywhere. The first thing I saw was the wooden butterfly broken in half, beyond that the little spoon and next to it the mirror shattered and little pieces of glass scattered everywhere. It looked like my make-up had been knocked over.

Although I had a knot in my chest, instead of letting the mirror be I slowly picked it up so not to cut myself, and that was the worst. I felt an electric shock through my entire body and had to lean upon the floor because I thought I was going to be sick. My face looked like it had been cut into strips, all split, and my eyes focused on the ceiling. I began to say the Lord's Prayer. I opened the closet. Between a rock and hard place. I didn't want to take much, but nor did I want to abandon things haphazardly there in Gualeguaychú. I was just about to pack my twelve Barbies but in the end only took one, Jocelyn, the dark one, the one in worst shape. The right leg completely torn off and missing her left foot.

Very confused. I could hear the desperate moans of Celia, our former Paraguayan maid, sprawled on the kitchen floor writhing in pain. I felt cornered, on the edge of an abyss, and then…Amen, I saw him, smiling on the cover of the CD "Ricky Martin" as if the world hadn't changed at all. I kissed him and then let's go. I didn't want to take any other memory. Besides, my backpack was filled to bursting.

After half an hour, not hearing any movement, I put my ear against the door of her room and shouted, "Mama!" Nothing. Louder: "Mama!" Silence. I felt like something terrible had happened. I looked for another key—in my house every door had the same lock—and then I encountered the scene. She was lying in bed with her arms opened wide, a half-empty glass of whiskey in one hand and the little box of Valium squished into a ball on the nightstand. She had taken all the pills in one gulp and was laid out like a crucifix.

I went up to the dresser on tiptoe. I didn't want to make any noise just in case my mother came to. On one of the walls, hanging by a thumbtack, was a photo of my sister when we were about six. She was smiling with her angelic face, all dressed up in a parrot costume with colorful wings. Without thinking twice I yanked it off and put in in my pocket while taking the opportunity to grab a silk scarf that I loved; above it was an enormous poster of the pop singer Jairo and not one picture of me.

I looked through all the perfume boxes and hit the jackpot when I picked up the Anais-Anais. Lately mama had become very suspicious and changed her "safe" every week. There were two rolls of bills tied with a rubber band around them. "Bingo," I thought, and instantly had an image of freedom and behind me the Obelisk and I could see myself standing off to the side, the happy ruler of my own life, wearing a fabulous orange t-shirt with a gigantic picture of Ricky's face on it. I left all the bottles in perfect order and before taking off wrote her a note: "I'll never forgive you. Don't look for me because you'll only be sorry. I hate you." Then I signed my name in all capital letters and kissed her on the forehead as if she were dead. I took her glass of whiskey and tossed it down in one gulp.

I fled with the two keys, $1,385 US dollars, and the perfume in my hand. Thank God before I left I noticed the hair dryer was melting over the telephone. A little black thread of smoke began to rise and I think in another second it would have burst into flames. Outside, complete darkness.

Gloria was in the street, sitting on the fence gate in front of her house; when she saw me coming out she walked over to meet me. It was about 7. "I called you," she said super bitchy, and me, "You talked to my mom?" and her, "Yeah" and then she scolded me because she'd been left hanging on the phone. "I'm sorry," I said, "but when I tell you what happened you're not even going to remember your name," and I didn't say another word until we were locked behind the door of her room.

I told her that Benito had raped me and then fled, that mama tried to kill me and I hated her, and I asked her to come along, we'd go to Nélida Doménico's and see all Ricky's concerts we wanted but she replied that she didn't have any money, nor was there any work for a gimp in the capital; she said she was sorry and we cried our eyes out because we felt it might be the last time we ever saw each other, but at a couple minutes before 10 I saw her skipping down the station platform holding her *equeco*, a cornucopia doll, wearing a red beret and with a backpack on her shoulders.

We got right on the bus and I didn't rest easy until they closed the door. We shut the curtains; I tried not to look at anybody, with my suitcase between my legs pretending to search for something, squatting and going through my stuff until I found my dark Barbie. Then I showed her to Gloria and said, "Jocelyn is going to bring us good luck." Tears were rolling down my face. I couldn't stop thinking about my sister and the dying face of my mother. By now the police had probably broken down the door and taken her off to the county hospital to have her stomach pumped. Two minutes before seeing Gloria I thought to call an ambulance, disguising my voice by covering the phone with the silk scarf. "I wish to remain anonymous," I said, "and report a suicide," and my voice cracked but I was still able to give my address and repeat three times for them to hurry up. I couldn't abandon her even though she deserved it. Seeing her like that tore at my soul, but I felt much sorrier for myself.

When the motor finally started I felt like I was lifting off on an airplane, grasping the armrests, my eyes closed, enjoying reality without her and glimmering salvation.

Gloria had already lifted the newspaper from the fat guy sitting across the aisle who told her he was a masseur and worked at the Buenos Aires Sheraton. Fat as a pig, he said he remembered her and her mother and he looked at Gloria biting his lower lip. A slimeball. I asked him if he'd ever seen Ricky. And when he told me no I stopped paying any attention to him. Gloria, too, but you could tell the idiot really liked us because he gave us his phone number in case we needed anything and she kept it without saying a word.

Although I closed my eyes with all the strength in the world, it was impossible to stop thinking; even worse, if I opened them Gloria would make me sick with her damned habit of explaining every item in the news. The only time she ever talked was when she read the newspaper. Nothing but criticism. Otherwise a tomb.

A little later came a guy asking for tickets and we had to look through all our bags because she couldn't find hers. Distracted as ever she'd put it in her beret, and if it hadn't been for the masseur we never would've found it. "Thanks," she said in a little girl voice, and him, "Forget it, it's just I saw it when you put it on," and you could tell he liked girls with no tits because he kept looking at hers.

"Give me the entertainment section," I told her, "and the classifieds, too, because we have to look for work." She didn't have either, but she showed me an ad in the first section, "for your Barbie," she said and elbowed me so I'd take a closer look. I read "Doll Clinic," wrote down the address and phone number and it seemed to me, at that moment, we would find a solution to all our problems.

The ticket taker came back toward the front of the bus and from his back pocket stuck out a kind of big metal soup spoon like the one from my house. The lights went off and we were left in the darkness. I remembered the photo of my sister I'd put in my pocket and ripped it into a thousand pieces while the driver waited at the last stoplight before turning onto State Highway 12. We sped up.

I swear to God at that moment I felt freer than ever, as if my lungs had suddenly become unclogged. I saw myself with the goods, with all the strength to get my first job in the capital, have a baby with Ricky, and be happy once and for all.

Gloria turned on the light, settled in with the paper and thirty seconds later said, "Tomorrow Princess Di's coming." And me, "Big deal. But luckily we're getting there first," and I recalled when mama had compared me to the princess. It was one time when she appeared in *People* and I was just about to turn thirteen and she had on a black corduroy hat and behind her was the name of the English school she used to attend, with her insipid hairstyle cut the length and width of her vegetarian face. The comparison didn't do me any favor.

Gloria broke through my hatred: "If Princess Di finds out the airport doesn't have radar, she's not coming," and she went on talking by herself. The light fell directly onto the paper, illuminating the face of the princess. I opened the curtains. In the middle of the countryside no need to be incognito. The moon was almost full, and the palm trees: as golden as in the opening credits of "Lord and Master." It was a special night and we were going to reach Buenos Aires at 3:30 a.m. Gloria asked me, "What do you have to do to become an illustrious citizen?"

"I have no idea," I replied. "I smell something funny." And I began sniffing our things until I came to the *equeco*. "That's it," I pointed with great certainty, not touching it because the thing already gave me the creeps and then she stuck it into a nylon bag. "I want to be an illustrious citizen," the poor creature told me. I replied I wanted to be a princess and began spreading cream on the dry skin of my legs.

Later I wrote my name on the seat in front of me with a red pen and kept going over it until the letters were carved into the plastic. While looking at the finished word "Esperanza," or "Hope," after Gloria had recounted step by step the tragedy at the military factory in Río Tercero, Córdoba, I thought that if I exploded or found myself involved in another tragedy, my name would remain here forever; I got a whiff of the *equeco*, although it was stowed in a nylon bag. And I dreamt of Princess Di. That she met us at the Retiro bus station, that she gave us her medal recognizing her as an illustrious citizen and that the three of us went to the Sheraton for a soda and despite her wearing the same corduroy hat from the photo in *People*, I really liked her and had to admit mama was right. We shared a certain air. A violent wind.

2

I'm the only Hóberal in the Gualeguaychú phone directory and everybody mispronounces my last name. "Hoberól," they say with an "o" and the accent on the last syllable and I correct them, nodding my head and emphasizing the accent on the first syllable. "Hóberal," I say, smiling and raising my eyebrows, realizing I don't care about the mistake. Trying not to reveal I don't give a shit if they mispronounce it.

I was born on the same day and almost at the same time as the famous Legrand sisters, Silvia and Mirta. We're all three Pisces and we've been branded by destiny. Risk-takers, fatalistic (so human!), but made of iron, and although born in different years (me in '77) our lives have way too many coincidences. We have a lot more things in common than being ruled by the same planets.

I also had a twin sister, but she died in an accident, so now I really don't have anybody to compare myself with. She'd surely now be rickety and skinny, but who knows. People get fat all of a sudden. I was also thin as a rail, but at twelve or thirteen I got fat as a cow. My sister probably wouldn't have been like that, she had a guardian angel and so probably would have stayed in shape.

She was born first, and as nobody knew my mother was expecting twins, they left me to be poisoned in the placenta inside her while my sister drew the attention of every nurse on the ward. She looked like a little doll.

The midwife grabbed her by the feet, wrapped her up in a towel, lifted her into the air and promised her a successful career as an actress in a mini-series and brought her over to the "Radiolandia" poster hanging on a wall. An enormous photo of Mirta Legrand autographed in black ink saying, "For the girls in Intensive Care, with all the love they deserve," and below that her name and farther down "A big kiss!"

"What a beautiful coincidence," said the midwife looking at the clock while counting on her fingers and saying how because there was only seven minutes difference between the time of Mirta's birth and that of my sister they might have the same ascending sign. And she recalled meeting Legrand at the Channel 7 studios when she went with her daughter to compete in "Carnavalísima '76."

The city of Buenos Aires had invited several groups from the provinces, and Julio Roca Avenue, festooned for the occasion, was filled with regional pride. Her daughter had been chosen to appear on Mirta's program along with some other girls, and they danced for three minutes at the end of lunch. The midwife was on the sound stage and she gave Mirta a kiss and had her sign the poster. The nurses all nodded like sheep remembering how great it was to have her come back to work the next day with such a dedication. They said "television" as if they were speaking about God. They were all so excited.

17

And mama screaming, "Nurse, I'm still having contractions!" completely abandoned with her legs still apart; then the midwife looked at my mother, bowed her head, crossed herself while arching her eyebrows, as if pushing the bad omen off towards the First Aid kit hanging from one of the walls with only half the red cross painted in the middle of the cover. Outside the worst storm of the summer was raging and you could hear doors slamming and interrupted sighs through the torrential downpour.

The patients at the Sanatorium de la Piedad fled from the rising waters of the Uruguay River that threatened the rest of the province. They had lost everything and the hope of returning home dwindled with the storm. The last thing they needed was rain and people enjoyed frightening them by comparing it to the flood of '76.

Nélida Doménico, the wife of papa's cousin who traveled there especially for my birth, says that what began as a normal birth turned into an inferno. That my relatives had to go into the delivery room to take shelter from the rain and that my mother was like out of it, turned rigid as if she were having spasms. She'd gotten a bit of peace and quiet after I was out, but it only lasted a few minutes and then she fell into a cerebral semi-coma for almost four hours that left as a result headaches that would torture her for the rest of her life. The midwives were afraid she was going to bleed out on them, but everyone's attention was focused on me.

They were still amazed I survived because I had remained way too long in my mother. They pressed on my chest to clean my lungs and as little as I was, I spit amniotic fluid out of my mouth. Moreover, they were afraid I might have strangled on the cord. Five minutes is a long time and nobody can take that much. Except for me, who doing honor to my sign withstood it all, as I've always taken everything in my life, with an iron will.

The wind was so strong that to get out of the delivery room they had to extend a tarp from one end to the other and used it as a roof to protect us from the rain. They wrapped us up in blankets and formed a human chain that accompanied us the whole way, like a procession.

The radio announced there would be no Carnaval celebrations that night, not only in Entre Ríos, but they also suspended them in the next province Corrientes and Brazil's festival seemed marked by misfortune: forty-nine dead and thousands injured. We passed down the corridors as if carried along by the steps of the crowd that covered us beneath the plastic until we reached the hospital room they had prepared for us at the last minute.

When they pushed open the door to our room the windows swung to from the gust of air, banging into the Venetian blinds, and the railing, loose for who knows how long, fell into the air.

Ten feet below, the midwife who had foreseen success for my sister in a soap opera decided at that moment to go over to the pharmacy across the street to get serum. She was wearing her little white hat, ready to take her first step, when the bronze railing split her skull open.

Traffic was stopped for several blocks around by all the people who crowded in to look at the corpse. It had been a long time since anything so sinister had taken place in Gualeguaychú, and the midwife's head, cleaved in two with her brain oozing over the hospital's sidewalk, was frozen in the collective eye of the town, which as soon as the storm let up came right over to see things live and direct. Thousands of umbrellas paraded through the door of the Sanatorium de la Piedad the day of my birth, as if the midwife's corpse were the body of some princess.

That was the first time I appeared in the news, in the media, when I was five hours old. If you look really close at the article in *The Gualeguaychú Herald* with the photo of the midwife sprawled in the street below the name of the hospital, you can see Nélida Doménico in the second floor window wearing a long Peruvian linen shirt with an asymmetrical neckline that was all the rage then, holding me in her arms. She's standing straight as a ruler, barely leaning on the sawhorse marked "Danger" between black and yellow stripes that the police had put up in the room. And then me with my face of a newborn, my gaze fixed on the heavens, tiny and lost as any baby.

For a long time the framed photo hung on the wall of my room when I lived in Gualeguaychú. And next to it, as always, a life-size poster of Ricky when he was with Menudo. I love Ricky Martin! He opens his mouth and it's like his words bore into my head. I tremble. I close my legs and force myself to think of something else or I get dizzy. My system shuts down. I get all light-headed and lose my composure. I can't do anything else but think of him and start imagining him inch by inch and automatically I take his clothes off and think of him inside me and I completely recreate him, perceiving him with my entire body until I'm about to explode, and that's when I lose control of my hands.

Ever since I was a little girl, mama has remarked to me the advantage of being composed. "You above all," she'd say to me, "because of how horny you are." And she explained how it was normal that when a twin died the feelings in the other would double, in everything. "Control," and she'd touch her forehead with her open palm, lowering her hand to her chin. "Con-trol," we'd both repeat before the mirror in my room as if we were saying just another prayer.

My twin sister blew up at age seven and for a long time they didn't talk of anything else in Gualeguaychú. Channel 9 and ATC came, and Channel 13 sent "Mónica Presents." There was an article in the Paraguayan magazine *Real Life Cases*. They published a photo of our house that looked like it had been bombed and next to it a really small wallet-sized picture of my sister and me, with an arrow pointing to the one of us who had been disintegrated. But they made a mistake and the arrow was directed at me.

The day of the explosion mama had gone to have a cup of tea with the taxi drivers on the next block; my sister was taking a nap and I was playing alone in the garden, alone as always, because even when my twin was awake it was impossible to play anything with her. She got dressed up as a peasant, an Indian, a bird, she would recite four very long poems by rote, flapping her wings. "'*Queo, queo*,' goes the flock of parrots, coming from who knows where," she'd say dressed in her parrot costume with colorful wings, and then change her voice, "'*Queo, queo*,' echoes the ravine." And if there was a party at home, twenty minutes of reciting and flapping wings and then the typical quick pass through the dining room; she was never quiet, she looked like a butterfly in slow motion and my father loved her more than life itself, following her without losing a single movement, always taking pictures of her; I admit flashbulbs left me blinded and in a bad mood. I couldn't do anything but show my album of butterflies while with disinterest I stated their scientific names. And not very gracefully. People would applaud unenthusiastically. Nobody picked me up in their arms and a moment later no more questions and that's all folks, because they'd already tired of me. It was all her fault. I hated her. That's why I was playing alone in the garden, because I couldn't stand taking a nap with that dwarf.

And suddenly the most beautiful butterfly flies completely around the patio and comes to rest upon the rubber tree. Huge, with black spots and wings with moles that looked like velvet. It was so hard to catch that I flew to mama's room to find a pin because I was afraid I'd crush it if I grabbed it by hand.

I approached as slowly as I could until just an inch away and when it opened its wings completely I nailed it right in the middle with the pin. It closed its wings, spread them again and moved its head from side to side at the same time shuddering in spasms.Then it remained stretched out and quiet. Perfect.

Urgently I went to hide it in my room.

My sister was sleeping near the stove, her cheeks colored orange from the reflection and her face all happy. I never understood why if we were identical twins she looked more beautiful, arching her brow, as if her features were pointed upwards. The most delicate nose. Besides, when she smiled her face lit up and she could buy anybody with that smile; mine nevertheless…well, all my features, even at the happiest moments, turned downwards. Crash diving. And so I grabbed my butterfly album and took off.

But before going out, idiot that I am I tripped on the gas line to the stove. I stumbled. The album went flying through the air and I had to put out my hands so I wouldn't fall face-down against the floor. The new butterfly was destroyed. My sister was sleeping with her mouth open as if she were disconnected, distant from pain and suffering, while my knees hurt from the blow; my anguish about the broken corpse in my hand wouldn't cease. I knew I'd never find another like it and this one had no more wings.

Something smelled rotten. I thought it might be the little body of the broken butterfly and when I brought it to my nose I realized that had nothing to do with it, and my immutable sister with her angelic face was submerged in sleep, in another dimension; filled with hate, I saw her at that moment more pallid than ever.

As the smell started becoming unbearable, after gathering the wings left crushed on the floor, after smoothing out the sheets in my black photo album that said "My Butterflies" in embossed letters, and after crossing myself in face of my sins, I went over to my neighbor's house so she could help me put the wings back together.

The clock on her dining room wall was fabulous; on the tip of the second hand was a wild butterfly and on the base little electrifying red roses and white chrysanthemums. It said "High Class Quartz" in black letters and on the upper part were two plastic golden lions. I could sit there for hours watching the butterfly go around.

Forty-five minutes later we were still in the dining room reassembling the wings with Super Glue when we heard the explosion. The blinds trembled, the clock fell to the floor and the lights went out. My neighbor began screaming and touched her heart. "That was at the gas station," she said, and her husband ran to the front yard to take a look while we stayed there still, dying with fear. Praying. And me, "What happened, Doña Angelita?" my voice catching like Andrea del Boca's in "Daddy Heart." The neighbor hugged me with all her might trying to protect me and I told her my chest hurt, and then we heard another loud noise.

Her husband returned, his face completely distraught. Everything had blown up. The gas had reached such a concentration that it was enough for my father, coming home from work ground down by fatigue, to turn on the light in the dining room for the house to blow into the air, and with it half my family.

Soon a crowd of gawkers congregated around the rubble; the trees in front had turned black and lost their canopies, looking like burned-out matches. The red light of the fire truck lit the street as if with flashes of light. You couldn't see anything, but you could feel an even murmur, disjointed and respectful, that only accompanies misfortune.

They shut me up in the neighbor's house so I wouldn't be traumatized. They made me recite an entire rosary along with five mysteries and then right into an ambulance to La Piedad along with my mother. Nothing had happened to her. She was saved by a miracle. She was lucky, because one of her clients had cancelled an appointment and when the cab drivers from the next street over brought her home, because though she was only a block and a half away she always made them bring her right to the door, nothing of ours was left. And nothing is nothing.

We went off in the ambulance; through the transparent cross in one of the doors I could see Inés Saralegui, a reporter from Municipal Radio, moving her lips in front of the microphone and looking at the place of my childhood as if it were possessed. The journalist became smaller and smaller in the center of the cross and at that moment

I felt I'd been left all alone, that I was the la
that the only thing left to us in this world w
phone book listing that read:
HÓBERAL PEDRO Rosario 436..............

3

My first job in the capital turned out to be a fraud and disgrace. I managed to get hired as a trainee at the Downtown Homeopathic Clinic and accepted giving up my first two paychecks for their slimming anti-cellulite treatment. I already had under my belt an endless list of bad experiences with my body and they promised me the definitive solution I needed for when I saw Ricky at his mega-concert on 9 de Julio Avenue. Besides I was really down after getting rejected by the Anamá Ferreira Modeling School and then at the casting of Alan Parker's film *Evita*, in which I'd placed all my hopes. But it ended up a disaster: besides not taking off a gram, they fucked me over because I left there fatter than I started and their flyers said that if I didn't lose weight, they'd refund my money. What a lie.

Finally after making a huge stink gathering evidence and showing up with Nélida Doménico's lawyer, they claimed lack of volition on my part and barely gave me back half, and then deducted sales tax. But it didn't end there. They made me sign a paper giving them full authorization to use the photographs they took before I started the treatment. It never occurred to me what they were capable of doing.

The photo appeared in the May '96 *Clarín* magazine. I appear in profile to my knees, with my arms raised above my head. My face isn't very clear because the color is bad quality, but my sagging belly yes. Above me is a little sign saying "Before" which I seem to be holding up with my hands. There's another really skinny girl who looks a lot like me, dressed in the same black thong, completing the ad. A clear and plain public humiliation that I'd certainly have to hide in the future. A stain.

I swore I'd carry the secret to my grave. They had me in a bind because I couldn't even consider denouncing them and once again exposing myself and feeling the camera flash bounce off my nude body. I would have committed suicide first. And I felt like that a long time, disconsolate and fearful of going out in the street, panicked I'd be recognized and a person on the bus would comment in a loud voice, "There's the 'before' photo from the *Clarín* ad." I would have died because I'm about something else, not about someone pointing their finger at me.

With the cash the clinic gave back to me, I bought a Polaroid camera and decided to wipe the slate clean, forget the subject and close forever the pages of the chapter "Downtown Homeopathic Clinic" in the book of my life. It would pass into oblivion like a black dot. Nothing more. That's what Liz Taylor said when she got out of rehab the first time, and I had it underlined in fluorescent marker in my hardbound Success notebook.

With that Polaroid 2000 I took the greatest photos of Ricky in October '96 when he sang on 9 de Julio Avenue. I'm so anxious that I can't stand the torture of waiting to get them developed; I want him there with me right now, so I can look and say to him I'd been there with him, the two of us frozen in that instant. Sometimes I framed the photos with my fingers so that the two of us would appear in the same image. And 9 de Julio Avenue more crowded than ever, they say, not even during protests. What a concert.

Gloria and I had contacted the girls in his fan club and we were all together at the airport to meet him Thursday, the 31st, and they helped me unfurl the banner in front of the Obelisk and later at the Sheraton Park Tower. A little more than fifteen feet of love. It said, "Enrique José Martín Morales: I love you," and it was signed Esperanza in red and yellow letters, all in capitals; I had pasted on two golden stars, one before and one after my name, which took up more than half the space.

Telefé had erected a giant screen at the end of Corrientes Avenue and at one moment they had an aerial shot of my banner in mega-scale, and I almost died of excitement. My name sat there so big that I couldn't do anything but scream. We were all howling. My legs trembled; from above we looked like two hundred thousand Argentine girls packed around the Obelisk with the Colón and Broadway Theaters as our witnesses.

When they projected the first images, Ricky's head was so big he looked like a god. It was an electric charge, a blessing, a storm of love, almost a miracle. Me, all revved up, looking at the pictures and unable to keep still, and all the girls around going crazy. Not for nothing; he was wearing the tightest corduroy suit, a white shirt and black sunglasses. That was his third change of wardrobe. He did five in all. I felt like I was getting wet. I was wearing really tight pants and began walking around in circles like a caged lion. I didn't know what to do or where to go, but I could imagine what was coming; a tingling in my pants and between my legs, moving like a straight line up my back and making me tremble, but concentrated with the fury of a thunderstorm in my zipper. I pulled it down while I kept walking, the girls looking at the gigantic screen as if it showed the image of God live and direct. Enormous. And me making my way through the crowd, trying not to get lost but unable to think. Desperate. Looking at the photos I had taken in the middle of the plaza and listening to him say to me "take me in your arms" and repeating it, all sweaty and hugging the air up on the stage, bowing low and holding his hands out to the crowd who went crazier than ever. The entire avenue began jumping all at once and the collective emotion was so intense that I began screaming with pleasure from feeling that Ricky's hands, which I saw before me incredible in size, would never stop, holding me everywhere like the girl in *King Kong*, singing "I Loved You" in my ear and my ear alone. He puts a finger to his mouth, touches the microphone and seems to kiss it. He's drenched in sweat. They focus in on him, I see him in the Polaroid, give him a kiss and feeling rather shameless manage to come just as the song ends. Me fulfilled and happy, him bowing his head to receive the applause.

It took me more than an hour to find the girls again and when we hugged it was pure energy. The concert had been an absolute success and we were all so happy for him. All crying, we stood guard there in front of his hotel until 3:30 in the afternoon the next day, which was when the press conference started. Complete madness.

At one moment I lost track of Gloria and began chatting with Marisa Mellman, president of the Ricky Martin

Fan Club, who told me about all her encounters with him. Seven times total. I hated her for that, but I couldn't stop listening and asking her to tell me all the details one by one, in order to see if she'd got as close to him as I had. I let her talk more than forty minutes, waiting very patiently for her to finish so I could recount *my* encounter with him in Gualeguaychú. And I was just about to tell her when Gloria showed up all crazy, grabbing me by the arm and dragging me away from the group. All super mysterious, she wouldn't say a word. She led me towards a side entrance where there weren't many people and there signaling to us both was the fat masseur from the bus we had taken to flee Gualeguaychú.

The press conference was about to start and he said something in the ear of a security guard, gave him a wink and pointed for us to take the red carpet through the main entrance of the auditorium at the same time Ricky came through a side door. I was petrified. They put us in the last row. A ton of people and cameras everywhere. I couldn't believe it. He was hardly fifty feet away, and for us alone because the conference was only for journalists and there wasn't a trace of any of the other girls from the Ricky Martin Fan Club.

For more than an hour of questions I sat there quietly, but then I raised my hand and waited for my turn a complete ball of nerves, Gloria elbowing me in the ribs, "What are you going to ask him?" and me silent as a tomb.

When they passed me the microphone, I thought I'd die and my voice quavering barely managed to get out if he remembered me. He squinted to get a better look and asked, "What paper are you with?" and I stood and said,

"My name is Esperanza. I met you in Gualeguaychú and saved your life," and he frowned, looked at someone in the front row and right then the earth fell out from under me because instead of remembering and thanking me again, he smiled and said, "To be honest, I don't remember." And the jerk next to him said, "So many times they've saved your life." Everyone burst out laughing. It was a lot for me to take. I couldn't believe it; they took the microphone and everybody looked at me out of the corner of their eyes. Thank heavens someone else immediately asked him another question, the attention turned elsewhere and I calmed down, but it wasn't more than a few seconds before two men asked me for my press card; I didn't have one so they each grabbed me by the arm and asked me to please leave the auditorium. Gloria acted like she had nothing to do with me and turned the other way and the idiot taking me off squeezed my arm even harder, not letting go until we were out on the street. Luckily they took me out a side door because otherwise I would have been a laughingstock.

I took a walk as if nothing had happened but I almost had a rage attack along the way. My hands were cold and I saw myself reflected in a car window. For sure he didn't recognize me because of my hair. I pulled it back. What was happening to me was really serious and though I was all torn up I couldn't hate him. Thank God I had my Walkman and pressed play and "She's All I've Ever Had" began. My tears flowed; I was destroyed. "What's wrong?" Melissa Mellman asked, touching me on the shoulder and I hugged her and told her all about the encounter with Ricky in Gualeguaychú and of course I didn't mention the press conference and a moment later she asked,

"Why are you crying so much?" and I lied, "Because I'm so happy."

The sound of the helicopter coming to get him made our hearts throb. The girls who had got hold of his flight information fought among themselves for a taxi to the airport. "Are you coming?" Marisa shouted at me, and I replied, "I'm going to wait for Gloria," and I paced around for a while not knowing what to do. I only had one question: Why had he treated me so badly? "Why, Ricky?" I thought, and pressed play to be with him again although he didn't remember who I was. People were slowly coming out and I decided to cross over to the Plaza San Martín. From there a few girls emerged walking together in small groups toward the bus stop. I continued along. I hummed through the first few lines of "Love You for a Day," trying to recall the video, doing the same moves as the straight-haired blonde in it with him and stumbling a bit during the back-up singers' dance steps. I'd have to practice more to get it all down. And just as I press stop and start to rewind the song to go over my rehearsal I see the helicopter appear near the side of the Sheraton tower facing the plaza, passing right above me. I automatically raised my hands in the air to greet him. I took out my white handkerchief and didn't stop waiving it until I saw him disappear, almost all the way to the avenue. At that moment I felt it had all been a big misunderstanding and eventually he would ask me to forgive him and that would be the end of it.

Gloria deigned to show up at 9 that night. I never forgave her for that. As if nothing had happened, she showed me an ashtray that said "Sheraton" in gold letters. "You like it?" she asked, and I ignored her completely and said,

"Why didn't you leave at the end of the press conference?" and her, "I stayed to look around the hotel." And about to explode I told her fatso could have done something so they wouldn't have thrown me out and she snapped back, "Damian couldn't do anything at all," and she emptied her purse on the table and out fell a pile of little containers of caramel they served at breakfast. And she told me she was going to study to be a masseuse at a school owned by the fat guy's brother-in-law in Devoto. I almost puked.

I was just about to ask her to please leave, that she not take it the wrong way but I needed to be alone for a while, when the phone rang and the operator gave me the big news.

Gloria seemed blessed by the angels. She was the winner on "Dream Gift": Ricky's shirt offered as a prize in the *Soap Opera World* contest. Impeccably white, which he wore at the concert and two days later they gave it to her in a gorgeous Armani box, tied with blue lace ribbon around the wrapping paper. The only thing you had to do to win was complete the form with legible handwriting and deposit it in the box at the entrance of the magazine offices or send it in by mail and wait, along with the almost thirteen thousand other of us girls who entered; Gloria, who had only sent in one form, won the prize. What an injustice. I spent a fortune buying a bunch of copies of the same issue, but it's obvious when luck is on your side all you need is a touch of the magic wand and there you go.

During the award ceremony Gloria was very emotional and that softened me up. We hugged at the magazine and ended up crying in each other's arms. Totally reconciled, but the photographer kindly asked me to move over a little because they needed a full-length shot of only Gloria for the magazine. They asked her to take out the shirt and she held it to her chest as if she were wearing it and I looked the other way because the flashbulbs really hurt my eyes; the security guard had these unbelievable arms and up above were three small TV monitors: one where you could see Gloria, small; on the other side me, and I raised my hand in greeting; and the middle one showing the magazine office's revolving door moving, constantly pushed by all the fans.

4

I met my best friend Gloria Diana De Biasio in '84 when we moved to a new neighborhood in Gualeguaychú because of the explosion that left me almost without a family, but she had already seen me on television a few times. That's because the news on every channel covered us. We were on the front page of half the newspapers in the country. Moreover someone started a collection for the "Entre Ríos Disaster Relief Fund" and we ended up receiving all kinds of donations. Boxes came from Salto and Paysandú, and our neighboring sister province of Corrientes came through like nobody else. A married couple that had lost their little daughter not long before in a similar event gave us a bed with an enormous butterfly carved on the headboard. An exquisite piece of furniture that became mine only because they'd heard me say in one of the reports that I loved butterflies. I learned at a young age that nothing is better than television for requesting things, and I couldn't believe that from then on everything was going to be for me and me alone.

When my sister was alive, I always got the worst for being the ugliest. The mended dress, the sock with a hole in it, the bare doll, the hard mattress. But that was before. My new bed came with a matching nightstand whose drawer handles were little daisies, the rest of the piece covered with butterflies. We had it all. Personally I didn't miss her in the least; after she died I closed the door on her memory, threw away the key, and began to be the queen of my new house and my new life.

My past life was left destroyed. As unrecognizable as the body of my father after the explosion. We had to have a closed casket for him at the wake but at least we found him and could mourn over him; there wasn't anything left of my sister. She blew up completely, with her toys and our clothes. Miraculously the only thing saved besides our car was a bronze chandelier Nélida Doménico had given my parents as a wedding gift, which ended up hanging from a tree as if it had been placed there by Jesus Christ himself. Perfect, straight, with the light bulbs unbroken and not a scratch on it. The tabloids really milked that chandelier. A cover of the magazine *Real Life Cases* described it as "supernatural" and a few people said they'd seen it illuminated, just the way it was with the cord cut, plugged into nothing more than the avocado tree.

One of the people who said she saw the "illumination" was Gloria's mother. They lived kitty-corner across the street from us, and the day we moved in, while the movers were still unloading our donated furniture, Hilda De Biasio recounted the episode to us with a luxury of details. She had learned news of the explosion its same afternoon but she couldn't come. Later that night, a tightness in her chest kept her from sleeping and she got up to take a diuretic an hour earlier than usual, around 5 o'clock. She was restless, a zombie, and at one moment grabbed her bike, rode into a fog and there drew a circle in the air with her right arm. She automatically found herself amidst the ruins of the house, not remembering how she'd gotten there. She couldn't stop moving her hands. "I felt it here, in my palms," she said, "as if they had nails driven through them." She confessed that only happened to her when an angel died, and the last part of the phrase she said in a whisper, bowing her head as if fearing to disturb who knows whom. Gloria looked at me out of the corner of her eye.

Her mother seemed inspired and became even more enthusiastic as she recounted how between the glass drops of the chandelier she could see a triangle of fluorescent light just ten feet away. "The miracle," and she couldn't contain her emotion. She took off her shoes to walk through the ruins not caring whether there was broken glass or exposed nails. Her jaw and chest trembling. Three doves from the eaves of the neighbor's house came and flew around the lamp, moving the glass drops. She seemed to hear music, her eyes were cloudy with tears, and the doves moved directly into what she believed was the presence of the Holy Trinity, "never absent," she then remarked, motioning with her head and arms, "from the funerals of angels." Mama looked at her entranced.

Gloria signaled for me to follow her and we went over to her house. She wanted to show me the little Guinea pig her father had found near the children's hospital and truthfully it was a horrible little thing. It looked like a hairy, tailless rat. "So why do you call it Spencer?" I asked. "See?" she said, lifting it up and showing me the chestnut fur. It really looked like a spencer jacket with buttons and everything. Carelessly placed in a cardboard box at the back of the entrance foyer, just where the staircase descended near a picture of Our Lady of Lourdes hanging on the wall like a sanctuary with a little roof over it, surrounded by candles and plastic flowers of every color. There was also a doll brimming with little nylon bags and I asked her, "What's that?"

"The *equeco*," and she told me she wasn't from Gualeguaychú, but that the year before they'd come from Salta and there this little doll of abundance brings you luck, touching her chest and crossing her arms like her mother.

We went to take a walk around the block, Gloria holding Spencer in her arms. She had perfect legs and a nice round butt. She told me her mother was obsessed with finding proof to corroborate a miracle, which was a family tradition. Her grandmother had tried the same thing and managed to accumulate the six indispensable requirements for an act to be considered a miracle, but when she finally had done everything the Episcopal Conference added a new one, rejecting the miracle, and her heart couldn't take it.

"Your mother is so intense!" I told her.

"And yours is so pretty!" she replied, shrugging her shoulders and, I don't know why, I felt sorry for her. She was kind of short and stocky but very angelic, with a little face like a Latin American Barbie. The blue t-shirt matched her eyes. Her only defect: a high-pitched voice. It didn't go along with her at all, and so she tried not to talk. She always acted the quiet one and me spilling my guts. I showed her my heart and she used to listen with interest to me, her eyes opened wide and a dumb look on her face, agreeing with everything I said.

We became friends immediately and began to see each other every day. We would meet after school to watch "Two Lives and One Destiny," with Rita Terranova and Juan Leyrado. Inseparable, even at dance time. We were the same age, both just as unpopular at school, and at that time counted between the two of us a collection of six hundred sixty-five photos of Menudo. But only I had an autograph of each member. Nélida Doménico got them for me when she saw the whole group by chance at a hotel in the United States; they're personally dedicated to me, and while they were triumphing throughout the world, I kept the autographs locked in my desk and let very few people see them. Gloria was one.

We'd almost finished our walk around the block when it occurred to her that I take Spencer and show him to mama; although it made me a little nauseous I agreed. I was scared to hold on too tightly because it seemed kind of squishy and the stupid thing escaped from my arms. It took off like a shot towards the street, and unfortunately just then a taxi was going by and thanks to me letting out a desperate scream, the swarthy guy inside managed to screech to a halt. Gloria was ashen. There were skid marks in the middle of the street and the driver got right out to see what had happened, but we never saw Spencer again. "It must have been scared out of its mind and escaped this way. You'll find him," he said, pointing right towards the sewer grate at the same time he extended his hand to my mother who'd coming running up along with Gloria's.

"Benito, at your service," and his voice was so raspy that mama invited him for a drink in order to put the unfortunate experience behind him.

After that mama made an enviable recovery. She was born to have someone at her side. And if he was young all the better. Six months after the explosion Benito had taught her how to drive; when my mother received the insurance payout for the catastrophe, they bought a Renault 12 for a business partnership and he left the taxi company. Technically, that is, because he still spent most of the day there. He came home around 11 and I had to go immediately to bed. My room is right off the dining room, where the television is, and I could see perfectly what they were doing.

Benito looked just like the guy on McGyver, only dark. He was black everywhere and they rolled around on the sofa and mama had to bite the pillow not to scream. Or if not he put it in her mouth and that was only time she shut up. Though they turned off the lights you could see them in the reflection of the television, and the embers of the cigarettes they lit every once in a while cast an orange glow over them like a laser beam. I would get cross-eyed from straining my eyes so much in the dark.

When Gloria slept over she couldn't believe how strong Benito was. She compared him to her father and felt like crying. "You're so lucky," she told me. We couldn't sleep from all our restlessness and we embraced each other trying to imitate Benito and my mother.

Gloria's father was a photographer from Corrientes, a drunk with half a finger cut off, and her mother gave dance lessons in the garage. "Classical, folkloric and ballroom" stated the hand-painted sign hanging on the door of the Academy De Biasio.

We were the best students there and usually danced as partners because we looked good together. Her swarthy and me fair. We danced so well that we both ended up auditioning for the lead in our school's end-of-the-year performance. We were in fifth grade and each wanted to be Sissy Empress.

Gloria got to dance first, because we were going in alphabetical order. She tied her little shoes again and again, biting her fingernails and scratching herself all over. She couldn't sit still, but her nerves left as soon as taking the stage, where she felt sure of herself. Instinctively she would stick out her butt and looked two years older. She regained her poise and moreover that afternoon danced like never before. Even my mother applauded. But while Gloria was leaping like a gazelle about the stage, mama whispered in my ear they were going to give the role to me because her parents certainly didn't have the money to buy her the dress. A really expensive costume for the role of the empress, made completely of tulle, the bottom ruffled and the lining all taffeta, with dangling pearls, not to mention satin gloves and a crown. "They can't even pay their electric bill," she said and began clapping. It was true because Gloria's mother was always complaining she didn't earn enough from the Academy and so had to work extra jobs, like reading coffee grounds or Tarot cards, undoing evil spells and even talking with the dead.

It came my turn to dance. Mama had put my hair in a bun and I looked like a classical ballerina, but I began to tremble. Every time I went on stage the same thing happened. I couldn't feel my legs and my heart went a thousand miles per hour. I believed my sister wanted to take control of my body because she couldn't stand that I too could move gracefully, and that although dead she was watching me from some place in the universe, and so the only way to escape her grasp was to shake myself until I felt I had gotten her off me. But that afternoon she was relentless. She almost didn't let me dance and in the end they gave the roll to Gloria.

My mother couldn't believe it. She looked at me with daggers in her eyes, but she didn't say anything. She had a whiskey in the cafeteria and sat there ten minutes smoking before she gathered her strength and went to talk with the school principal. "She's the only daughter I have left," she said, "and I need to see her dressed as Sissy. For me it'll be as if…" and here her voice cracked, "You know about my other girl, no?" And she lifted my chin with her hand so the other woman could better appreciate me. And when she had gathered herself, she said, "That other girl can't be a princess. When has there ever been such a dark Sissy, and with such a shrill voice," and seeing what was coming, I begged her, "Please don't cry, mama," but she didn't pay any attention and although the principal also shed a tear, the roll still went to Gloria, at least for that day. The principal had the satisfaction of showing us the portrait of Sissy Empress with jet black hair all in curls that fell below her shoulders. "How ugly," mama commented as she passed her hand over my loser's straight hair lightened with chamomile.

With that sadness, she recounted to me that when she was pregnant she would hold upon her tummy a fabulous photo she had taken when she'd been crowned Queen of Carnaval in '73, where's she all in white wearing a diadem of spectacular fake diamonds. She would concentrate then on her stomach so that the grace which had led her to ride atop the float and three years in a row be named a baton twirler would fill us in her womb. And she'd caress my hair and tell me she loved me.

The only time my mother ever paid attention to me was when she cried. I'd be so happy and we'd hug, but then she'd keep drinking and get really mad when I asked her to stop, above all when I dumped the bottle down the kitchen sink and then slaps and shouting and things would end up badly.

A little later while talking on the phone with a client, thinking I had gone to play at Gloria's, she confessed that I'd never amount to anything, that all the natural talent a baton twirler needed my sister had possessed and she even spoke of divine injustice, referring to which of us two the Lord had decided to carry off to heaven, and she began crying again as if nothing could calm her.

That afternoon Gloria and I made a pact as sisters. We stuck our left thumbs with a compass, joined our blood, looked each other in the eye and swore friendship for the rest of our lives, although she danced better than I did and my mother hated her for having won the roll of Sissy. We held our fingers together; on the television raged a ferocious storm with thunder and lightening. We were watching an episode of "Charlie's Angels," our favorite show. Sabrina and Kelly were trapped in the middle of a storm.

That same day returning from the market, we raced down Almafuerte Avenue. She was winning as always. Besides I'd just put on my new stockings and I didn't want to wreck them. At the corner of Ponteagudo, Gloria began to run faster to take the lead on me and just then I saw the most extraordinary little orange butterfly and of course I got distracted and stopped a second to look at it but Gloria kept running as fast as she could and then I had to shout with all the strength of my lungs, "Sabrina, no!" because I heard the motor of a car coming full speed and had the worst feeling; the idiot looked back like in a close-up shot and, I don't understand how, she tripped, did a perfect somersault in the middle of the street and a Mercedes Benz with Buenos Aires license plates hit her at the moment she landed, running over her right leg with two tires. Then it took off, leaving her face down and open-armed.

Gloria wore a cast for six months, had another year of physical therapy, and was left with a shattered femur. And there happened what had to happen: since she couldn't play the empress, they offered me the role.

"I and the spirit of my daughters are here," my mother told the principal. She wore a black suit with shoulder pads that made her look super slender. Dark glasses, make-up on up to her ass and her hair in a French twist that turned into a snake-like braid, an image right out of *Glamour*. A princess with a black satin purse applauding in the first row on the verge of tears. And not for nothing. The play was a complete success. The whole town in the theater. They carried Gloria in and sat her down right in front with her crutches next to her. Her legs didn't hurt so much anymore but her neck was quite stiff and although she still had her wrist bandaged, at one moment she raised the thumb we had stuck; I did the same and it was our secret greeting from the audience to the stage. She got all teary. So did I.

My costume wasn't missing anything. I even had pearls incrusted in the plaits of my hair; the hairstyle from the epoch, though I looked more like the girl in "Flashdance" than an empress. Mama's work, and she came in euphoric and sat down next to Gloria's mother and thanks to that they began to get along better. Especially when she learned that besides reading Tarot cards and meeting with the Holy Trinity, Hilda De Biasio also communicated with the dead. At the time she'd started drinking again and half the day heard the voice of my sister reciting. Or she would be sitting there all calm after shaving her legs and suddenly hear some desperate creature's cry and she'd shout "Fire! Fire!" and it would be Benito in the kitchen who had just lit a match. And that's how in our house matches, the brazier, and any little knick-knack with a flame were banned and from then on we only used a sparker.

5

I wanted to be the first to have Ricky's latest CD and the only way to do that was ditching school. At first bell, Chorus, the only record shop in Gualeguaychú that carried decent merchandise, was about to open.

I had to walk around the block so Gloria's mother wouldn't see me leaving home. I was incognita, and she, in the street, a dust rag in hand, was talking to a neighbor but keeping tabs on the block's every movement. I waited a moment and took advantage of a couple old ladies walking by to jump between them and sneak past. It was just an ordinary morning but, I don't know why, I had the feeling that all of Gualeguaychú was out on the street. And suddenly the entire town changed into a huge witness ready to testify against me.

At 8:55 I was hidden behind the flag pole in the municipal square, watching the blinds in the windows of Chorus, as nervous as if I were attending the world premiere of a Hollywood movie.

I was wearing a pleated skirt cinched with an elastic waistband and a long-sleeved blouse; I was standing behind the flag pole because my school was just about to have its first recess. Chorus was located right across from the entrance, and if they spotted me they would call mama and get me in big trouble. She only let me miss school when I faked being sick, lurched around as if I had stomach cramps, contracted my muscles and then, a moment later, came down with a fever. And moved, my mother would let me go on sleeping.

That morning I had the blanket pulled up to my nose, a suffering look on my face, with a cup of garlic tea to lower my temperature. She was super fresh with all her batteries charged. Mama's problem was the afternoons, after 6 when she didn't have any more clients; during the two or three hours she waited for Benito she got really anxious, and first she had one drink to relax, but then another, and another and another and another. And now, if there's something to give her credit for it's that the next day, as fresh as a daisy, she'd get up at 7:30 to do aerobics with the work-out program on TV. From a distance she and the host María Amachástegui looked like twins, and besides, they wore the same sweat suit.

"I'll be back in about an hour," she said and promised to bring me a Mydol. When she touched my forehead I asked her if the fragrance she was wearing was the new perfume Nélida Doménico had sent her. She answered yes and pronounced the name as it was written, smelling her other hand: Anais-Anais. Nélida had also sent a divine imported cosmetics case full of little compartments and I always suspected that it was really a gift for me and that my mother, with no qualms at all, had openly kept it for herself. Thank God eventually I learned I was right. I don't like to mistrust someone for nothing.

Shut up in the back of the house, mama was oblivious to everything. In the mornings she only did depilation and in the afternoons nails and make-up. She had to start very early, because according to her that was the best time to work. "After midday the pores close and the skin gets damaged," she used to say. Besides, with her clients she freed herself of all negative energy and concentrated so much on each one that she averaged at least fifty-five minutes per appointment. Plenty of time.

At one moment I saw someone coming to the school door to look outside. I couldn't see very well who, but when she got a bit closer I realized it was Gloria. After the accident she was on crutches for six months. They took her to a specialist who told them, "If you want the girl to walk correctly, she needs reconstructive surgery. That's the only way." And she had to get used to limping. All the family could do was console her: if they won the lotto they'd even out her legs. "If there's any money left over we'll fix your nose," her mother told me, and she ended up working at the Eucharist of Christ in search of help for her daughter.

As for me, I was always right there for her, bringing her homework every day, devoting the whole afternoon just to her. Gloria loved *Stories for Veronica*, but she couldn't hold the book and so I opened it to the page she'd left off at; and I would've gladly read to her, but she wouldn't shut up about me reading without pausing and a ton of other things, because she always had something to criticize. We also filled out the questionnaires that come in women's magazines, and once we did one to measure friendship and she killed me because she gave me a 2 in geniality and a 1 in camaraderie and besides lowering the score as friend those grades didn't make me happy at all. But that's how Gloria was. Unpredictable, and although quite a bit of time had passed since the crash, she still had trouble walking.

Now she took a few more steps and crossed the street, looking restless. She couldn't risk getting another reprimand, because she'd already received ten. She stopped in the middle of Almafuerte Avenue and scanned all around the plaza as if she were the Bionic Woman, but of course she didn't see me, quiet as a mouse behind the flag pole.

The day before, at the last minute as we were leaving school, I told her we would buy the CD together and blah, blah, blah, but I couldn't wait I was so anxious; and knowing me, she knew I'd be there right at 9 to be the first and only one to have it.

My heart stopped. While trying to evade Gloria, the biology teacher almost saw me. She wore a frighteningly bitter face. Pale as ever and thank God in a hurry and distracted; if not, she'd have seen me. At the last moment I managed to turn around and leaned back against the pole, doing nothing to draw attention, super natural. Gloria had disappeared, luckily, and I could breathe easier. Besides, without the school uniform you looked older. As the teacher passed by with her stone face, wearing a horrible silver broach and carrying a black briefcase, I bitched out Gloria and her damned habit of spying. Keeping out of her sight, I snagged the nylon on my right leg on a wire and got a run to my knee. They were my favorite stockings. New Queen Christinas, very fine quality, that had cost me an arm and a leg and made my legs look really thin. I swear for a moment I hated her.

Just when the bell rang to return to class, my teacher climbed the steps up to the entrance with her hair in a perfect black bun; as if it were all timed, I heard the motor of the gates at Chorus and imagined the curtain on paradise being raised.

I crossed the street hunched over, hiding my face with my hair. Back then I wore it long and straight because I wanted to look just like Catherine Fullop in "Abigail." And as I was looking down the first thing I saw was his chin and three-day stubble on the promotional poster; an immense, glistening mouth, his eyes wide open like all Capricorns. I had to control myself not to scream; Titina, the sales clerk, had already seen me and she pointed at it with her super long aqua green fingernails.

Without taking my hand from the door handle, I shouted at her, "Hurry up! They're going to see me," but I couldn't help looking at the school and I'm sure I saw Gloria quickly ducking her head like an ostrich.

I went in and pleaded, "Please, Titina, play it already!" We wasted almost ten minutes because the idiot couldn't figure out how to turn on the stereo until finally it blasted out of every corner and in every hole of our bodies and, since everything was all right, we started screaming at the same time and both ended up crying at the end of the first song. Although she'd cried a ton, she still looked impeccable because she was wearing a Tsu foundation on her skin that seemed to me the max, and the cover of the CD drove me crazy and I could only stay and hear three more songs because it was already 9:20, just enough time to get back in bed and under the covers and hear mama coming up the stairs all exhausted.

"What bugs me most about Ester," she said, "is that she leaves my head throbbing, she has her negative energy all in Mars. Very dense," and she took the thermometer out of its case and said, "Lift your leg, baby," and she wet it a bit with spit and stuck it in my ass. Me quiet as a mouse. She touched my forehead. "I'm sure your temp has gone up," and she went to make me a cup of tea because she cured everything with infusions.

With the thermometer inserted the wait seemed eternal. I had Ricky's CD under the sheets and the new Madonna and Luis Miguel, who in reality I didn't like at all, but when Titina got crazy I could get away with anything and so taking advantage of the situation I grabbed whatever was in reach and that was all I could get my hands on.

"You're all sweaty," mama said to me when she came back, and not for nothing. 100 degrees. She shook the thermometer to lower the temperature and then that damn habit of sniffing it and saying, "OK!" I shouted at her, "Don't be a pig, mama!" and she took a Mydol out of her pocket and put in my mouth. Just in case, I swallowed it. I was all excited and had to wait ten minutes for her next client to arrive so I could finally hear the last nine songs.

Mydol knocks me out. When I woke up mama was talking to Celia in the kitchen. She'd been with us almost a month, and though she'd come with recommendations I didn't like her at all. She seemed dirty, a smart mouth. Despite mama making her wash every morning with lye soap, she gave off the sensation of not being clean, period. I'm sure she looked through my drawers and in the month she was with us ruined three of my t-shirts. And besides, each time Gloria came over she made her wait in the street. I finally couldn't take it any longer and shouted at her, "Dumb bitch!" and she responded "Welfare queen!" It was simply too much. I detested her saying that to me, because it's what they used to write on our street door, referring to the monthly stipend we received for the catastrophe that mama managed to get thanks to a "connection" at city hall. I left her there talking to herself, wishing her the worst, and whenever I saw the opportunity to show her whose house it really was there was nothing she could do but be left with the mote in her eye.

We used to watch "Abigail," and she was a fan of "Poor Little Devil," which was on at the same time, so she couldn't watch it. At first she begged me to got over to Gloria's, but as I told her a million times, she was supposed to be working. And so as long as she was cleaning my house someone would have to tell her about the show later.

I couldn't stand her anymore. The morning I was "sick" she came to ask if I wanted her to straighten up my room but I forbade her to come in. I had unfolded the poster enclosed as a gift in the new CD and wanted to be alone with him for awhile. That huge mouth. His long wavy hair that was just killer. His eyes wide open and his ever-present smile. I loved it and ten minutes later I was already dying to hang it on my wall. Then to make a little space I decided to take down a few old photos of Menudo that I didn't like at all and took the little stepladder to put them on top of the armoire and came across the electric blue case where I used to keep my Barbies when I was a girl. It gave me the chills and I wanted to look at them again, with their dyed hair and party dresses and when I managed to grab the handle I felt something was wrong because the clasp was wide open and I never leave anything open. I took it down and scattered my Barbies on the floor, already having a bad feeling. Twelve in all, gifts from Nélida Doménico who bought them in the United States, and to the horror of my astounded eyes I found some without their little legs and others with the foot completely torn off and other signs of mistreatment.

At that moment a thousand things passed through my head and I could perfectly well imagine who was the author of such evil: I swear to God that I recreated in my mind the scene of her going in and could picture her twisting off each little foot and making them suffer one by one.

Holding the bag of Barbies, furious but completely silent, I went down the staircase separating the kitchen from the living room. Celia had her back to me listening to Radio Asunción, completely absorbed in the dishes. The announcer was giving the weather forecast for the weekend and then said, "It's 3:30 p.m. throughout the entire country." Stealthily walking with all my anger concentrated in my shoulders, I hit her right on the money with the case, screaming at her, "You fucking bitch!" and she fell to the floor while I continued beating her.

The story doesn't end there; when she recuperated, the traitor wanted to turn me in, but thanks to Benito having a friend at the police station she made a declaration they later threw in the wastebasket, and justice was served.

I called Gloria and she came flying over. She told me that a few days earlier Celia had wanted to talk to her mother, who wasn't home then, and that she had a strange bag in her hand. It seemed to her it might have been the feet of my Barbies.

And me, "Why didn't you say anything, Gloria?"

And her, "Because I wasn't sure and didn't want to blame anyone." And she began to cry.

I couldn't be consoled either, but I gathered my strength so I could tell her the details of the fight. The Paraguayan of course denied everything and even blamed Gloria. She couldn't believe it and she hugged me and we remembered when we first met, when we used to spend hours in front of the television with our dolls fixing their hair. She loved playing at being a stylist and I'd change their "look." She had her own doll, but it wasn't a real Barbie. Hers was a Tammy whose little dresses instead of fabric were made of some kind of plastic. And we'd play that Tammy was a country cousin visiting the modern city girls with school uniforms, new dresses and different hairstyles, who transformed her into a pop supermodel.

Later, when things had calmed down, we swore our eternal friendship and vowed to defend ourselves against anyone who ever tried to come between us. And though Gloria had a very strange look in her eyes, she kissed me on the mouth and I let her.

6

It was Nélida Doménico who finally opened for me the gates to television and gave me my first decent job. She had an agency in Montserrat where she cast extras for soap operas, hostesses for events and laughing audience members for programs: August 13, 1997, I walked onto a sound stage for the first time. I remember shooting a whole roll of twelve taking pictures of everything, the microphones, the cameras, the sound board. I cried. It seemed like I was daydreaming. I was really excited. I was wearing super tight pants. A huge cloth purse with two packages of candy, a hairdryer, and Gloria's fuchsia hat that matched my blouse I brought in case I had to change my look, but it seemed so loud I didn't have the courage to take it out of my purse. It was a hat just like the one I'd seen on Angélica Durán in the soap opera she was in before "The Condemned." I loved Angélica Durán, she always played the bad girl. One *TV Guide* cover had declared her "the woman of the 3 F's: fabulous, famous, and frivolous," but I admired her.

At times people confused me for her. Nélida Doménico told me I had the Durán flair, but not the nose. "I know already," I said, and her, "The identical hair." Then, as if it were a secret, lowering her voice although we were alone, she began, "The truth is, you're a little…" I stopped her short because I didn't need a comment like that at such a difficult time for me and I walked towards her with my hands on my hips: "I know already. Don't tell me. I'm doing everything possible," and her an angel changed the topic and complimented the make-up on my nose. Feeling bigger than life, I confessed to her my technique and passed on all my secrets, and her, "You're a doll just like your mother." I gave her such a dirty look she had to apologize, and me, "Forget it, it's nothing, but I'd prefer you not compare me to her," and I picked up a picture frame with her son that was on the shelf and said, "He looks just like…" and she cut me off, "Shhh!" pointing at the door with her finger and then at her ear, and we had to fill each other in because we both needed to know the smallest detail about everything. We were exactly alike that way.

"You look fantastic," she finally said and promised to give me another make-up case, lowering a bit the neckline on my t-shirt. Then right there she took a folder out of her desk and inside, placed in an envelope, was the photo that had appeared in *The Gualeguaychú Herald* showing her with me in her arms, leaning against the "Danger" barricade wearing her Peruvian blouse. "What a fantastic color that was," she said referring to her garment, and she told me how they don't make them like that anymore. "Another style," she added, showing me how badly they now fit in back. When I turned around to show her my own problem with my ass, she put her hand on my chin, lifted my face and said as if inspired by the stars, "I have a lot of faith in you, Esperancita," repeating "a lot," and her eyes filled with tears. "I see your name in lights," she said, opening her arms wide in the air, "*Esperanza Hóberal*," and she put my photo under the marquee she had drawn in the air. That's why she put me on Telefé's waiting list and a month later they called me for "The Condemned."

My first scene as an extra on the soundstage was at a table in the back of a bar. I was waiting anxiously for a man, Mr. "X," but a mirror showed my reflection almost in close-up. It didn't take much for me to get into character because my pants couldn't have been any tighter. I had to close the zipper little by little stretched out on my back. I didn't know how I had put them on in the morning. I was a bundle of nerves, and with the fuchsia blouse buttoned up to my neck I felt like I was choking. When they put on the red light and shouted for silence, I panicked and my hands trembled. The skinny guy in charge of the extras told me to pretend I was writing a letter in order to do something; if I couldn't do that I should scribble the name of the guy I was waiting for. "Do something with your hands," he instructed me and I obediently wrote an X the size of a bathtub that took up the whole page of my notebook and tried to fill the edges of the letter with little butterflies and flowers. I just couldn't take it. My glasses got all foggy and I began sweating like a pig. They had to stop the scene because of me. The skinny guy shouted through the loudspeaker, "Fix the make-up on the fat girl at Table 10. We can see the drops of sweat on her." I don't like the word sweat and his comment really irked me. It seemed out of place, but I learned that in the world of television that's the way things are and as I'd gotten the job because of a connection I didn't want to make a scene, especially before the cameras. I sat there on the bar stool until the make-up artist came to fix me up again. She wiped a cotton ball over my face and put on two brushes of color. There was a horrible silence in the studio, as if we were filming. I took the fuchsia hat out of my handbag and put it on without asking anybody. I retouched my nose with my own foundation, cast a frantic glance at the extras guy and that was that. I looked divine.

Luckily Angélica Durán wasn't in that scene or I would have died of shame. I'd just run into her in the bathroom on the third day of shooting. Fabulous. You could see they did her eyes in an almond shape to make her look even more evil. Me hypercool walked up to her and said a thousand things. She had fantastic skin. She complimented me on my hair, looked at herself forever in the mirror and then left.

As soon as she was gone I began to copy her gestures and posture. Where did she get so much grace, so much charisma? Pure production, because she wasn't pretty and only as tall as me. I covered the bump on my nose with a finger, trying the upright posture with my legs spread one a little ahead of the other, my tits just a bit pushed out in front and my chin neither raised nor lowered, but level.

At the end of filming I went up to her and asked if it were true she knew Ricky Martin. She responded she didn't like talking about it but said really humbly, "One of these days invite me for coffee and I'll tell you something." I really liked her, she was super nice, tender; I took a picture of her with my Polaroid, the last one that came as an extra in the roll of twelve that I'd saved especially for her. She looked divine. She's looking at the camera and her hair falls to the side as if she'd just got it styled. Her smile perfect and her teeth straight and white as snow.

That very afternoon I stuck it on my cork bulletin board and put a flower next to it. We were identical. Like two drops of water.

The next time I saw her she looked completely different. Dark glasses, her lips and nails painted a strange orange that nobody wore then in Buenos Aires, and a lilac hat with a diamond-shaped brim. She was going over her lines with her assistant. An absolute diva.

I entered through the revolving door a complete wreck, hyperanxious, and out of pure chance I was wearing around my neck a wide brilliant violet velvet ribbon, almost like Angélica's, but louder. I put it on so that people's gaze would go right to it. From there to my tits was only down a couple inches; and when they were done checking me out, my boobs would have already flashed them. Now if it occurred to anybody to start with my ass I was lost. It was impossible to make my hips smaller. Not even the slimming band that did everyone wonders did anything for me: I was allergic to it and got a red stripe around my waist that looked like a ringworm. At that point I already believed I'd been damned, left traumatized after what had happened at the Downtown Homeopathic Clinic. Besides after crying nine hours in a row without taking a breath in front Ricky's poster from feeling how much I loved him, from being so anguished not to have him by my side, from having to bear that black hole that had settled in my chest and at times seemed to expand like the one in the ozone layer, without any hope of getting better, all I could do was eat and eat and eat. And that's why I'd devoured a half-dozen pastries and the latest *TV Guide* on the way to the station. The new one had come out that morning and was in my purse, wet with tears.

When I saw the two of them off to the side of the main set I was petrified, I couldn't even go down to the lockers to leave my things. At that moment I wanted to go up to Durán and yank the script out of her hands and scream whether it was true what *TV Guide* was saying.

"All the extras of 'The Condemned' to Studio 3," came over the loudspeakers just at the moment I decided to approach her. "Table 10," the make-up artist shouted at me (that's what the people on the set had baptized me after the incident at the bar), "did you see a ghost?" And then I came to, frozen like a statue five feet from the revolving door. "They're waiting for you in the studio," she continued and gestured with her hands for me to hurry up. "And don't even try talking to that one," she said, pointing at Durán, "because her dressing room is flooded and she's acting crazy."

"You have no idea how I am," I said to her, but she'd already gone off and didn't hear me. I had to gather all my strength to get to Studio 3. They were waiting for me.

When we finished shooting she still had a couple of scenes left. Time enough to eat something and go to the station's parking garage. I bought six empanadas and wolfed them down. I wiped my hands on the roof of her car and sat down to wait. I took the *TV Guide* out of my purse and could do nothing but look at her photo and hate her. I couldn't stop thinking about what I was going to say to her, and how she'd take it. I felt lost, I'd have to rehearse my words in advance because the last time with Ricky hadn't turned out so well. I began to go over in my mind the famous phrases in my little notebook, but none seemed too convincing.

The advertisement for ATT (Advanced Thermal Therapy) took up the whole backside of the front cover and I started to fill out the form. I had to do something with my body. Marisa Mellman had told me it was really good and she managed to lose ten pounds without any effort. The model had circles drawn around the problem zones. Mine: eight in all. At that moment I realized that with my build it would cost me double the money, as each four points raised the price. The next page in the *TV Guide* was a sign. This disgrace could befall anyone. Even Rafaela Carrá was out of shape, and I didn't want to end up like that. Durán appeared on each page like a hologram, inviting me for coffee, and Ricky at the disco in Gualeguaychú telling me, "Thanks, sweetheart," giving me a totally wet kiss and then taking off. And later at the press conference, "So many times they've saved my life," with everyone bursting out laughing. And Angélica wasn't coming and me with a thousand questions.

Besides I wanted to ask her, and this had nothing to do with the magazine, if it was true she did drugs. That's what Irma, the station's make-up artist and the only nice person at that place, told me. She recounted how at times when she was working on Durán's face she had to give her a massage to make her relax a little. "Famous, frail, and fucked up," she said, recalling the article in *TV Guide*. Irma never shut up; she mixed colors with her brush, gathered her strength and went on criticizing. When somebody crossed her she let loose with everything. She gossiped that on a couple occasions she'd had to give her a twelve-milligram dose of Valium so she'd stop grinding her teeth. I don't understand very well why but I preferred her to tell me about Ricky. She'd done his

61

make-up seven times. Seven, like Marisa Mellman! It seemed too much. I would've died. At that moment I wanted to be a make-up artist. To think that I'd had him to myself only one time at the disco in Gualeguaychú and I was in heaven.

"Divine," Irma said, bringing me back to reality. "Randy."

"What's 'randy'?" I asked, and her, "Sexy, girl." And she bit her lip and gazed into the mirror as if she were looking at him. I did, too.

"And you know who took his virginity?" she went on, and right then I lost my breath. I wasn't sure I wanted to know, afraid I wouldn't be able to take it, but my lips repeated tremblingly, "Who?" "An Argentine, girl," and she went on doing my make-up but I was no longer paying any attention. I started going through all the photos I held in memory to see who it could have been, and at the end of the search all fingers pointed to just one person.

Angélica saw me in the parking garage and gave a start. She came floating along. Alone, luckily. Not a hair out of place. She was perfect. Her lips retouched, her shoulders straight. A complete change of clothing. A checked jacket in a turquoise that on anybody else would make you puke but on her looked fantastic. There are people born to wear any rag at all and look splendid. Angélica Durán was one of them.

"You're from the station," she said to me, almost asking, and took off her glasses.

"Of course," I replied. I couldn't believe she didn't remember who I was. I'm quite noticeable and people remember me. "I'm Esperanza Hóberal. I'm in the program and the other day we were talking in the bathroom and you told me I should invite you for a cup of coffee…"

And her with a face like she was on the moon: "Excuse me, but I don't remember having told you anything. Besides, I don't like to talk about my private life with people I don't know," and at the "I don't know" she paused, making a movement with her head that if I'd been next to her would've been straightened out with a punch. "Control," I thought, gazing firmly at her and that same horse face she made in "The Condemned."

Angélica had a terrible voice. She was the one who had hinted to me about the coffee, and now that I took her up on the offer her stardom surfaced. I came around because the car was between us and stood next to her; she couldn't find her keys. "Calm down," I told her. "The only thing I want to know is whether it's true." I put my hand in my purse and she remained there with her almond-shaped eyes wide open; then I grabbed the *TV Guide* and showed her the photo of her leaving the Sheraton's parking garage. And the yellow letters asking, "Who's Durán Visiting?"

"That's all lies," she defended herself while digging though her super expensive bottomless black purse. In the desperate attempt to find her keys, an envelope fell to the ground. Instinctively I bent down and didn't resist the temptation to read all I could. It said, "Two Invitations," and to one side the logo of Chakira, a discotheque in Palermo. I began to tie things together. Irma had told me that later that evening there was going to be a party at a disco; she didn't recall which but was sure there was a "k" someplace in the name. I grabbed her by the wrist and said, "Are you going to the party or not?" while I pointed at her with the envelope I held in the other hand.

Then after a struggle she said, "Get out of here, kid," and opened the car door with an ease and grace that split my soul with envy. Before she got in she spat out "crazy," which struck me deep in my heart. Then she locked the car, started the engine and kept honking the horn so that I had to escape like a fugitive through the service door. But I had the pleasure of shouting "drug addict" at her and pounding three times on the hood before running off. Luckily I kept the invitations.

I arrived home blinded with fury. My head was spinning. I had walked back from the station and it was quite late. On the way I'd eaten three more empanadas. I couldn't stop thinking about her and wishing her the worst. One more second beside her and I'd have ripped her earrings right off. How could it be that one day she was so nice, so together, and the next day we see each other her mask falls and that diva in the station garage appears? "You don't play around with me, Angélica Durán," I thought, putting some rollers in my hair as if I were on automatic pilot, beside myself, dragging around the entire house that hate Durán had produced in my body. I couldn't keep still. I began to straighten up the kitchen unable to concentrate; her stupid face appeared on the box of matches, on the kettle, in the Knorr soup, saying, "I don't know you" in her little nasal voice. "I don't like to talk about my life."

"You should have chosen another profession," I shouted at the package of tea. I couldn't believe she had called me crazy. "Look, there are a lot of things to scream at somebody, but that...that, no!" And I went on talking to her as if she were there before me. I felt oppressed in the kitchen so went into the laundryroom. I needed to keep busy, to do something, and right at that moment Angélica's two pupils turned into the two o's in "control." I was getting paranoid. I grabbed the robe I'd just ironed and went running to the bedroom, fleeing from myself.

When I turn the light on in my bedroom and see her nice little face from a couple days earlier on the corkboard and I look at myself in the mirror, I realize with anguish springing from my eyes that I don't look like her or anybody I know, the drug addict smiling in the Polaroid, a green thumbtack stuck in its white edge. Then copying the fake professional smile, I go up to it, press down on a corner of the photo with the tip of my thumb, and with the other hand all at once rip it in two. Just like that.

I swear to God I heard the sound of breaking glass and saw how her head smashed against something metal and in the distance a siren began wailing at full blast. Right then I felt better. I could see more clearly, as if I'd put in eye drops; as light as after having cried fifteen hours in a row facing a poster of Ricky. Liberated.

I sat there looking at the corkboard, but without seeing her, gasping. I took a deep breath. "For me you died this very instant," I remember thinking, and I couldn't stop imagining her torn apart dressed in her checked jacket.

That's how I was, holding the photo, touching my heart, my head in the clouds, when the doorbell rang. I thought they were coming to arrest me. That for sure there was a camera in the garage and they'd filmed everything and the doorbell rang again and I ran into the kitchen, desperate, and opened the window I don't know why because I wasn't going to jump and the fluorescent lights of the ads on the street shimmering while I hear Gloria's voice shouting at me from outside and right then I remember she'd just come back from Gualeguaychú. Relieved, I took a breath and opened the door for her, a piece of the Polaroid in my hand.

"Isn't that the photo of Durán you had on your bulletin board?" was the first comment the bitch asked me. "No," I answered sharply and her, "Give me a hand," pointing to a moving hamper next to the elevator. "The lady on the third floor gave it to me," and me, "It's filthy," and I felt relieved she didn't ask anything else.

She was carrying a shoe box lined with gaudy tissue paper with orange and lilac diamonds. "What nice paper!" I exaggerated while pushing the hamper. "Durán has a hat with the same pattern." Then I said, "What is it?" trying to sound interested, and I don't know why but at that moment came to mind the image of the *saginata*, the cadaver of a coiled worm at the bottom of a bottle filled with formaldehyde in our eighth-grade biology text book, under the caption "Saginata Tapeworm," coiled like all dead worms in the bottle. Gloria brought me back to earth with "silly stuff," and took a little book from the box and told me she was thinking of making a list of all the clients she had, now that she had a practice and had done her first paid massage. And me, "Who?" and her, "The woman on the third floor."

She took off the windbreaker and under it she was wearing Ricky's Armani shirt that said "Exchange" in white letters next to the pocket. I couldn't believe she'd put it on to travel. "It's gorgeous," I said, touching it. Gloria smelled like a man's cologne. "Who were you with?" And her with an idiotic face, "Nobody. Damian brought me in his new truck." Then I told her Durán had invited me to a disco that night and was going to introduce me formally to Ricky. "Where?" she asked, taking my hand from her, incredulous and dying of hate.

"I'm sorry," I told her, "but I promised Angélica I wouldn't tell anybody." And I went into the bathroom. It was already getting late.

Of course I took my purse with me, in it were the invitations to Chakira and I couldn't trust Gloria at all. She'd changed so much she seemed Chinese. She was wearing cheap black rope-soled shoes. Even her eyes looked a little Oriental. If I hadn't known her my whole life I would have said that besides giving her an intensive course the fat guy had brainwashed her or something. She'd changed so much she didn't even want to wear her platform. Flat heels or espadrilles, there was no other choice. Mama would've died seeing her. Insipid, and the whole damn day talking about breathing and the body. And I had to live the entire day with my own and at that moment I didn't want to talk about it. Water struck my face; I remained in a nebulous vapor trying not to think.

Gloria opened the door and came into the bathroom. "I have to pee," she said and told me she'd seen my mother; I stopped her right there. "Don't tell me anything," I said, "just tell me if you did what I asked you," and she stopping pissing and after a pause answered yes and left without using the bidet. Very strange.

I sat there squatting, trying not to think. I'd asked Gloria to call home to talk with mama and without saying who it was leave this message: "If you'd been home the day of the explosion they would have been saved." Just that.

I finished my shower without the least idea what to wear. A total blank.

7

August 31, 1993, on exactly the ninth anniversary of the explosion, my twin sister communicated with mama through Hilda De Biasio in Gualeguaychú. It wasn't the first time they had tried to make contact, but they'd never managed to synchronize before and the sessions ended up a big nothing. Still, mama never gave up. After the poster of Hilda appeared at the bus station announcing her first sermon at the Temple of Christ, she began believing everything Hilda said, especially if it were related to the spiritual world, the theme of which, according to gossip around town, she was an expert.

Besides that the weather forecast for the thirty-first couldn't have been any better. That it was Friday, that it was the third attempt and that the Santa Rosa storm looked late in reaching us were all good omens for Hilda.

At 7:30 mama left home with a bottle of whiskey hidden in her purse. She was wearing a black and turquoise checked turban, a striped cotton turtleneck and wool slacks. How ridiculous. I acted like I didn't see her. She crossed the street and went into the academy. I waited a second to follow her. The sky was heavy. I asked Santa Rosa to please hold off the storm one more day, which was very important for me, but though I stared at the clouds with all my might, like I was trying to break them apart, I didn't have much faith at all in myself because the sky was starting to get quite dark.

Gloria was in the patio next to the staircase, sitting in her favorite place chewing her fingernails under Our Lady of Lourdes. "And mama?" I asked. "She's there," she responded, pointing her eyebrows at the upper floor where Hilda held her consultations. They'd wanted to redo that part of the house but left the work half done. Gloria slept in the master bedroom, which hadn't yet been plastered, and in the next room her mother talked to the dead.

I sat a step above her, even with the *equeco.* There was a strange smell, like a cemetery. I'd always preferred plastic flowers. At least they didn't make the house smell of wakes and as they were always bigger, at the same time they hid that hideous doll of fortune. Looking carefully at it up close it looked a little like Gloria's father, but I never told her that.

"Stop biting your nails," I said at one moment and she didn't say anything, reading Louise Hay's latest book as if it were a mystery novel. Then we heard, "Little girl, answer," coming from my mom in an unnecessarily loud voice. Gloria looked up. Then another scream passes through the door and the limits of my patience.

I hated it when mama caused a scene in someone else's house. I was just about to go up and tell her my sister was dead, to stop shouting, that the turban made her look old. But then Gloria, who saw me going, grabbed me by the hand and signaled we should go try on clothes in her mother's room, where there was a full-length mirror.

"You want some Tang?" she asked. "OK," I said, and her, "Get yourself a glass and one for me, too," and she went into the bathroom. Up until then everything divine, but when I sat up I don't know what movement I made, the thing is I stumbled forward. I had to lean on the little altar and barely managed to grab the vase, but not anything else, and the *equeco* fell into the air. My heart stopped. Every muscle in my face tensed and all I waited for was the sound of the little doll shattering on the floor, but thank God a bucket filled with dirty water was beneath it. I thanked Our Lady that Gloria hadn't seen me, quickly shook off the *equeco* and tried to arrange it behind the carnations so she wouldn't notice it had gotten wet.

I made us both Tang and sat there waiting in the kitchen. I washed my hands a couple times but despite everything they reeked of a vapor mixed of dust rag and Lysol. Horrible. When Gloria came out of the bathroom she had a frightening stench of cigarettes about her. Me with a nauseous look on my face, "Were you smoking?" and her, "Not at all." I stared at her because she knew very well what I thought of girls who smoked, but I had to swallow my words because I desperately needed her to lend me some clothes. Something completely killer for that night.

I'd already washed my hair and mama had plucked my eyebrows at 9:30 that morning, but I still had to do my nails. I couldn't believe how thin I looked. That was my best period. You could see sixteen in every part of my body. My tits were perky and although not the thinnest I've ever been, you could see my hip bones. I don't understand how I could stand going five days without eating. Lemon juice and tea. A goddess, but my face had thinned and cheekbones sharpened, making my nose stand out. I put a finger on the bridge and saw it wasn't really so bad compared to some of the clothes hangers you see around here, and with a bit of surgery it could quickly be fixed.

But for the time being I disguised it with make-up: the area to the side well defined, just a touch to the tip, a quick pass over the ridge, another beneath the nostrils, a lot of translucent powder, and the result was astonishing.

When Hilda finished the session with my mother she had dark circles under her eyes like she had been talking with Satan. Her hands were trembling and she had to lay down a minute on the bed while we tried on mini-skirts. I was very curious and asked her if she had made contact. "Yes," she said, completely out of it; I stood up straight. "What did she tell you, Hilda?" and with great patience, although half worn-out, she explained to me she had lent her body to my sister. "To the entity," she said, "but I lose my mind. I'm in a complete fog." She grabbed her head just like my mother did and her breathing became heavy, as if she couldn't get rid of the remains of my twin. Then Gloria and I asked her almost in unison, "Is it going to rain?" And she couldn't answer us because she'd fallen into a deep sleep.

During that contact my sister used Hilda's body first to recite a fantastic poem by Khalil Gibran and then accuse me of causing the explosion. "That woman is crazy," said Benito, who in a low voice called her "Radio Dead." And mama, kneeling in the middle of the dining room, looked at me and said, "I can't wait...if I have a..." and pronounced "killer" so out of the side of her mouth it was almost inaudible, "...daughter, I want to know right now, at this very moment," and she made the sign of the cross, bowing her head as if surrendering. The light from the dining room struck her full on the neck and all her hair was gathered under the turban. What a howl.

I'd already finished my make-up, was dressed, and had my nails half left to do. Benito had taken advantage of mama's distraction to slip out. He hated conflict and she went on repeating the same thing; she'd gotten up off the floor and now sat on the sofa, inspiring pity. My patience was running out. Drunk and crying at the same time: impossible to understand her, and I was already late and by now should have been ready. My nails were perfect, but I could still smell a bit that odor of grated cheese on my hands that reminded me of the *equeco* falling as if in slow motion without me being able to do anything about it. I said to mama, "Why don't you fix your make-up instead? It's run all over your face." Magic words. "You're right," she replied and turned her head to look at herself in the mirror. Then she asked, "And Benito?" surprised not to find him.

I couldn't wait any longer. At 10 Ramón was playing at the Church of Christ and I had to be there. It was going to be sensational, a brass band with drums, and Daniel Toro's sister had been invited to come. Me in a thong and super short black leather mini-skirt, slit on each side, and a plain t-shirt borrowed from Gloria's mother.

Hilda began working for the church cooperative, but in a short time was already part of the Eucharist of the Prayer. She suffered so well in public that in just three months she started to deliver the main evening sermon. Gloria, she and I had walked there together a little before services started. The three of us down Almafuerte Avenue, our backs straight and heads held high, Hilda rehearsing her sermon. We were the talk of the town as we passed the bus station, and then sat there at the church talking with the musicians and speakers, more than ten in all.

Ramón sang during almost all the breaks. The huskiest and most contagious voice in all Gualeguaychú facing all us girls Friday evening. To shouts he'd cry, "Halleluiah!" And the crowd, "We're on the road to salvation." Behind him a sign with blinking lights saying, "The glory of the Lord will embrace our hope." Enormous. I couldn't take my eyes off him. The green spotlight shown on Ramón's face, highlighting his prominent jaw. Then a new song began and he wiped his brow with the sleeve of his tight black rayon shirt, which looked killer on him. I couldn't keep still, biting my lip, making an effort to keep my knees together. Looking out the corner of her eye like always, Gloria pressed her hand on my leg whenever I was about to scream so I'd keep calm right at the exact moment.

I suspect she liked Ramón, too, but never wanted to confess it to me and so she kept it to herself, like she did with everything. Plotting alone and acting like the good girl. Deep down she knew Ramón would never pay any attention to her. He was looking at me. It was obvious, and I confirmed it that night in the church patio. When he finished singing I went with him while he had a cigarette. It was 11:30 and Gloria's mom had taken the stage. She was very intense and began exalted. "We are going to cleanse you of disgrace and corruption," she said, and that meant we had a break of fifteen minutes, more or less. Ramón didn't say anything to me, he just smoked looking at the stars. The band played music that chased away the Devil with their minds. I didn't do anything but repeat one sole wish and thank Santa Rosa for letting me have that joyous moment outside. Gloria appeared in the door and seeing we were sharing an intimate moment went away. She couldn't hide her butt face and disappeared. Her mother invoked the name of Satan and the people shouted as if they were throwing him out. The organ music really loud. Not a cloud in the sky.

When Ramón took the last drag, it was obvious my message hit the Universe of God and then he told me I had a half hour to congratulate him, and surprised I asked him why. I never forget anybody's birthday, much less his. He got all serious, then sat there thinking and told me it was his saint's day in a disappointed tone that made me feel horrible, and I wished I could have turned back time.

Taking advantage of my anguished moment, he grabbed me by the shoulders really hard and gave me a kiss. I felt his jaw inside my mouth, his arms around my back, and I fell in love with him for all he had done to win me over. Gloria's mother sounded louder than ever. "I feel somebody has cast a spell on you," she was saying. "You have been a victim of misfortune, brother." And in the background the organ music. The microphone was in Ramón's belt and he was squeezing me so much I felt like I was suffocating. "Satan, we are going to kill you and you will not return," I heard, and he passed his tongue over the roof of my mouth. And I thought to myself, "This can't be real." I couldn't believe what was happening. "Glory be to God. Ask for help and here I will be," said Hilda, and she began giving appointment times for the following week. We didn't have much time left. I was floating. I felt Ramón throughout my entire body. When he let me go, I saw it wasn't the microphone but his dick that was sticking out the top of his pants, purple and pulsating. I couldn't stop looking at it, hypnotized to the max, and then Gloria's mother appeared. "Ramón," she shouted at him with a gesture to hurry up, and he made a rapid movement; two seconds later he was back at his place and nobody noticed anything; I felt like he was my Six Million Dollar Man.

Hilda accompanied him back inside with no other comment than "button up your shirt, mister." And he dedicated a song to me from the stage. He didn't say a name or anything, but he said, "For you," raised his right arm and looked to where I was leaning against the wall, smelling my hands and remembering him in every inch of my palm. He was wearing a fabulous very sexy deodorant. I couldn't keep still. Nor could I find Gloria anywhere. I had to tell her everything. I had to spill my guts.

That night Ramón took me home and we talked at the door until 3:30 in the morning, which was when the storm finally let loose. He didn't stop kissing me. He was touching my tits the whole time. And you could see I was giving off something sexual, a kind of essence, because not only Ramón went crazy but the next day men turned to look at me when I crossed the street. Even something out of the ordinary happened to Benito.

I was laying on my bed trying to sleep a bit before my soap came on when mama came in holding the car keys and dressed as if she were going out, chewing gum; you could see in her face she'd been drinking. She had to drop off the orders to the Avon reps and after that had an appointment with Dr. Lottito, who I'm sure was going to prescribe something for her nerves and migraines. She had put on a horrendous shawl; mama wasn't a woman for shawls. A short neck. To top it off, every time she put on her make-up drunk she painted her lips smaller and aged ten years. "OK," I told her, "but Benito has to hook up the television here in my room." I felt like a pig, I'd eaten half a plate of noodles, and as that wasn't part of my diet the guilt was a thousand times worse. Besides Benito loved to be in charge of the television and anything to do with electricity.

Three minutes later he was in my room. He wasn't wearing a shirt and you could see the tattoo on his arms, a serpent coiling around a staff of life that resembled the logo for Union Pharmacy but which looked fantastic on him. Me, almost squatting, laying on my bed with my legs open. The soap opera had just begun, and when it was finally tuned in he settled down beside me. I grabbed the eyebrow tweezers and the little mirror. I told him, "Blow your smoke the other way." And him, "OK, OK," his voice real serious and smelling of cigarettes. And he tickled me to see if I'd lighten up. And me, "Idiot, knock it off."

I was watching the TV between my legs. Super concentrated, because later mama would ask me about all the details and she didn't want to miss anything: at what moment the main character cried, where he put his hand after kissing her, what expression she wore. But Benito had great abs and I wanted to look at them out of the corner of my eye. He left his cigarette butt standing on the night table, came close and motioned for me to give him the tweezers while he put his finger there and began to move it very softly. "Bunny rabbit," he said to me and my knees weakened and I got wet for the first time watching the beginning of "Señora."

Caridad Canelón was walking down the street in a short rabbit fur wrap, a style that looked good on her. She had a fabulous neck. Benito lowered his head, smelled between my legs and caressed the edge of my panties until he couldn't take it anymore and pulled them up with one finger. With the other hand he took the mirror from me, put it right where I could see myself and kissed me. In front

76

of me I could see his thick black hair and beyond it Canelón in the foreground. And then the commercial came on.

I felt seven million germs crawling over my body and couldn't keep still. Benito sat up with his zipper already down and told me to search inside. When I found it, he asked me to please smell it and brought the mirror closer so he could see me. His dick got enormous, and was the same color as Ramón's. I put my hands on his face and asked him if this wasn't a sin; he answered it was only a sin if he stuck it inside me, and then we heard mama's car parking in the garage and the motor turning off. My heart stopped. Benito jumped up and before leaving signaled me, putting his finger to his lips like one of those "Quiet" signs in a hospital, but with his McGyver face. Two seconds later he disappeared and I stayed there in bed not knowing what to do.

I tried to stand up and grabbed the wooden butterfly from the headboard with such force that it came off all in one piece, and though I tried to put it back in place, it was impossible.

When mama came in the room I was holding the butterfly in my hands. "What's wrong with you?" she asked.

"You don't see?" I snapped back in response. "And you?"

"Lottito didn't show up," she said and asked me to tell her about the soap opera. She was in a really bad mood. She grabbed the tweezers and the mirror, and sitting on the edge of my bed she evened out her eyebrows right there, while I made up step-by-step what had happened. It was like I was on the moon and I think I never came down again. My head was thick and I couldn't concentrate. "How strange!" she said to me, looking at the butterfly and scrunching her face as she began plucking. I was dying to smell my fingers and tried to without her noticing, thinking that in another month I'd turn seventeen. During the commercial she took the butterfly from my hands and tried to put it back in place; in her movement she brushed against the nightstand and the cigarette butt that was standing on the edge fell to the floor and rolled lost under my bed. "Benito!" she shouted, and him, nothing; silence.

8

What Benito said to me kept rolling around in my head and the next day I took advantage of the siesta to clear up my doubts.

We were at Gloria's house watching the end of "Señora." Absolutely starving. I'd decided to quit my diet and I downed by myself two packages of Duquesa cookies besides a pastry and a half, because Gloria hadn't wanted to finish hers. Her mother was mending a gaudy blouse next to the window, leaning toward the light. She looked tired.

Her suffering face made her look younger and although she was basting that turquoise blouse with small red pompoms that hurt your eyes, she looked fantastic. Every once in a while Gloria had to try it on; in the meantime she filed her nails with an evil look on her face. Her jaw was rigid like she was chewing on something. Besides being naturally disagreeable, Gloria was always uptight. I told her that all the time, but just to look sinewy and ripped, she lived with every muscle in her body tensed and stiffened. "You're going to stunt your growth," I told her a thousand and one times, but the dumbass never paid attention.

I was lying on my side facing the door of her father's studio, my neck super twisted, finishing plucking my eyebrows with the tweezers, and as he was always working at his desk, I didn't want to point my *cholila* that way. There was one cookie left in the package and I put the whole thing in my mouth, letting it disintegrate until it was just a paste on my palate. Duquesa was a relaxing part of my siesta, because when I watched that soap I got so nervous and fidgety that the only way to lower my anxiety a bit was by eating something sweet.

Her father was setting up a camera with a giant lupe adjusted on his head and had one eye covered with a black patch. Just like the guy on "Gilligan's Island." As serious and crabby as his daughter. He hadn't shaved in a few days and drop of sweat fell from the middle of his forehead.

In such a strategic position and my miniskirt tight everywhere, my back was killing me and then, when the program was over and I was stretching out, I asked Gloria's mother, my voice kind of low, if it were a sin if someone touched me, showing her with my right hand where I was referring to. She put down the blouse and Gloria tensed up even more. She responded, "Not at all," and asked why. Gloria snuggled up smaller on the sofa.

"Because I'm a woman," I answered, "and I don't want to make anyone mad, much less God." And I sat there looking at the ceiling, copying mama when she wanted to remember something. I loved it when I plucked those lines from Caridad Canelón copied down in my Success notebook, ideal to blurt out in situations like this. I repeated the phrase in a whisper.

"And if they suck you?" I asked Gloria softly. At that moment her father raised his head. His eye was a hundred times bigger behind the magnifying glass. Gloria sat up, fixed her eyes on me, and answered no. "It's not a sin!" she screamed at me without thinking. And her father got up to close the door as if he hadn't heard anything.

"Now if they come it is, stupid," Gloria said in my ear. And me, horrified, "What?"

"If they come in you, stupid," she repeated very seriously and puckering her lips she got in the same position as the blonde pig we had seen in the porno magazine her father kept under lock and key. Dyed blond hair and her tongue sticking out out like she was licking an ice cream, covered with jizz and all these guys around her beating off. My stomach turned just thinking about it.

"And how do you know?" I asked her.

"I read it in the Bible," she answered, and I believed her because her face didn't look like she was lying. "What are you two talking about?" asked her mother and she came over so Gloria could try on the blouse. And that's how the conversation ended, because I didn't have anything to say about the Bible. Besides, I didn't want to mess around with God.

I wanted to go into the boys' locker room with Ramón. We met every other day in the school bathroom when I had gym class, and we'd go into the back stall because it was the only one with a door and he loved to rub together like an animal. He was the perfect height and we stayed in there the forty-five minutes my class lasted.

Every once in awhile Ramón twisted his jaw to the side and the bone sounded as if it were broken.

"Factory defect," he joked and then squeezed me. Always the same way. I loved to feel him over my entire body, with that face of an orphaned calf that just killed me, and concentrating with his arms raised like he was being robbed, he would say, "Hands up," and lift his leg, press against my hips, and then the same thing over again. I loved it.

The day before my seventeenth birthday I promised him a very special gift. Him, super intrigued, asking me what I was going to give him, calling me a "dirty little whore," his zipper already down and his underpants showing; it was hard as a rock and pressed against my belly button. Quiet as ever because the stalls didn't have roofs and just in case someone came in it was better not to make any noise. He was pressing against me like never before, kissing my neck and telling me I was the most beautiful girl of them all, and when he was just about to reach my lips he stuck out his entire tongue and licked my mouth. I felt Ramón's hot legs against my body and his dick began to move, he got all red and I felt something wet, then I put my hand down and touched it all over my skirt and screamed at him with disgust, "Imbecile!" I couldn't help it. My palm was all sticky and I started to gag. Then we heard the voice of my biology teacher saying, "Who's in there?"

Ramón stuck his finger into my shoulder. We sat there frozen. Now knocking on the door, Natalia "Gossip" Parmessano said again, "Who's there?" We barely had time to straighten our clothes and open up because shouting like a hysteric she threatened to call the janitor and the principal. I tried to cover the stain with my folder, swearing, "What's that animal doing in the boys' room when she should be correcting biology tests? Old maid, sticking her nose in the bathroom where it doesn't belong." And she took us to the principal's office, checking out Ramon's legs the whole way, and then looking down at the floor as if she didn't want to see anything else. Me with my eyes on her black bun wishing it would explode.

Gloria was at the gymnasium window looking at us, like the whole tenth grade, while we went down the hallway that seemed endless to me at that moment, as if I'd fallen into a time tunnel, and a tunnel of shame.

A half hour alone in the principal's office trying to avoid the big mouth's face. I saw the word control written in fire with colored chalk on the wall before me and I saw her there standing up straight, upset, walking around wearing a horrendous orange sweater and a polka-dot skirt that couldn't have been in worse taste. And to fuel my hate even more, I fixed my gaze on her, remembering what she was like before she got separated, before her husband left her. Another person. Nothing at all like the viper there with us, with that ugly metal brooch in the shape of a worm she hadn't taken off since getting dumped. To the point she looked like she had a shrunken neck; and even more, she had terrible skin tone.

To think we had once gone together to Concepción, Uruguay, on our end-of-the-year trip, and she laughed the whole time. Really cool. Everyone in seventh grade chose her as our chaperone. Gloria and I had a photo of her with us at the San José Palace. "Let me take my bun out so I don't look so serious," she told us, tossing her hair back. When she took her glasses off she looked like Linda Carter. Her shoulders and the nape of her neck well defined.

I had tacked it up on the corkboard next to the photo of Ramón on the stage at church. There was also another of Gloria with her little girl face, but sticking out her butt and flat stomach, and one of Ricky when he was with Menudo. Fabulous. Young, thinner and handsome, with a broad face but sharp features and the jaw so marked that Ramón's was just the shadow of it.

When the principal arrived, the biology teacher disappeared. "How you'll fly off my corkboard," I thought watching her leave, as the principal set her glasses atop her head and put on her sermon face. "Get out of here now, mister," she said to Ramón. And when we were alone: "This can't be the end of this, Esperanza. You acted like a whore." And it was a long "whore," pursing her mouth. Me, nothing, not a sole word. "It's my duty…to ensure the incident goes beyond these four walls," she said touching the middle of her chest, and she wasn't lying.

Ten minutes after I got home the biology teacher was ringing the doorbell. I finished changing and hiding the skirt. I wanted to eliminate proof of the sin forever. I wanted to burn the thing, but it was the only denim skirt that made me look skinny and I looked fantastic in it. I'd also have to destroy the telephone bill. Luckily I grabbed it when I came in or mama would've given me the worst. It's that I hadn't withstood the temptation to call "Esperanza Gracia." She was fantastic, I saw her on cable on the Spanish television channel, where she began her program reading letters viewers had sent her, divining things on the air about their lives, envelope in hand. I wrote her a thousand times in Madrid, but she never read my letters on air. That's why when I heard that she was working in Buenos Aires, I decided to call her.

I couldn't believe I was talking to her, hearing her super strong unmistakable Spanish accent, and that increased my desire to know and explore and confront everything about myself. We talked for forty-five minutes and I was really excited. She said very concrete things about my past. I almost died when she asked if my family had suffered a tragedy or something like that. "An explosion," I said to help, and her, "Exactly," and she foresaw a change of life and environment for me. "Another horizon, Esperanza," pronouncing the "z" strongly, and it seemed to her a cosmic coincidence that we had the same name. She spoke very slowly, calmly. She conveyed a lot of peace, but now the bill had come to one hundred thirty-nine pesos and mama was going to have a heart attack. For that reason I thought about taking the money from her and going to pay it, because she never thought about the phone bill, or any other, if she didn't have it in front of her nose. And so everybody would have been happy, if it weren't for the biology teacher's orange sweater that stuck in my eye like a little piece of dirt.

"Esperanza, I have orders to talk with someone in your family," she said, sticking her hand out just in case I decided to slam the door and smash her face. The metal brooch had become unfastened and at any moment was going to fall off. And I shouted, "Mama, there's someone here for you."

"Who?" my mother said from the kitchen.

"An informer!" I shouted, looking her in the eye, and I went up to my room with all the hate one could muster for a human being deposited in the bones of that bitch.

I listened from behind the door. My room has a view of the whole dining room. Mama was wearing a fine-threaded blouse with fancy stitching and linen slacks. An absolute model. And I see the two of them about to sit down but my mother brightens up, compliments her on the polka dots and offers her a cup of tea. "Ah, no," says the bitch, raising her hand. And my mother, "The water's already hot." And Parmessano drops her hand like a marionette. I look up and see her photo with Gloria and me at the San José Palace on the corkboard and the hate is so great that I stand up and tear it right down. But the tack doesn't come out, the photo rips in half and the biology teacher is split right down the middle, as if she were a cell in plain process of mitosis.

At that moment I heard a desperate scream and then mama saying, "What's happening to you? What's wrong?" shrieking like she does when she gets agitated. My heart was going a thousand miles an hour. I went down the steps with the photo still in my hand. Flying. And then I see Parmessano sprawled on the floor dying, with her black bun half undone, her head going from side to side as if she were saying no at the same time she was having spasms.

You could tell the idiot hadn't seen the step you go down into the kitchen and tripped forward, falling with all the weight of her body. The pin on the brooch stuck her right in the middle of her heart. She lasted exactly two minutes; she closed her eyes, opened them again and then remained still, the nape of her neck all stiff. "Goodbye, Diana Prince," I thought when she stopped moving and I joined my wrists like Wonder Woman did with her anti-bullet bracelets when they shot at her. I felt stronger than any woman alive.

The first thing mama did was take a Valium with two fingers of whiskey. Then she called Gloria's mother on the phone. And the latter, when she stood at the bottom of the step just where the teacher had tripped, said, "It must still be here," stretching out her fingers as if trying to feel something.

Ninety minutes later there was a lot of people in my house. Gloria's dad brought his professional camera he'd just had fixed and took an impressive color photo. After that I began serving whiskey assisted by Benito, who amidst all the tumult had time to remark to me that what we'd done wasn't a sin. I acted like I didn't believe him because I really liked him following me all over the house. Parmessano had turned blue, and everyone commented that if the pin had stuck her a half-inch to the right she would have lived.

They drank three bottles in all; even Gloria who is anti-everything got a buzz. She went to look for an ice tray in the living room and that's why she's not in the photo. I'm alone, standing on the step with the body of Natalia Parmessano covered with a sheet in front of me and the metal tray I served the whiskies on held out so naturally it looked like an extension of my right hand. Feet together and back straight. "What presence!" I thought. To see that photo of me the next day in the newspaper was the best birthday present I got; with posture like mine I could only be a model. Nobody was going to stop me and eyeing my little notebook of sayings I found one Gloria had told me that I'd noted on the last page, where all my favorites were. It said that if one thinks something and rethinks it and doesn't stop reflecting on it, eventually it will become true; Louise Hay had written that. Next to it I'd noted the address of the Anamá Ferreira Modeling School, because that was the place where I wanted to study when I went to live in Buenos Aires. Esperanza Gracia had foreseen for me a "change of life and environment," and I couldn't wait until the moment I was finally there. In the middle of everything.

9

Two years before I left Gualeguaychú forever, Ricky Martin, who had just then begun to achieve success on his own, was in town incognito for the opening of Carnaval.

Of course, Gloria and I danced in the parade. Me first and her second baton twirler, which was really commendable, because she wore a platform on her right leg that completely evened her out. Even so you didn't see anything. The base, bordered with sequins and feathers, covered to the floor the five inches of wood. Mama took care to make sure it wasn't noticeable; she was beside us the whole evening taking care of every detail.

"Stand up straight. People can see the thong between your cheeks and your asshole is going to show," she said into my ear, and me moving my leg until she signaled with her head it was OK now. My panties were wedging into my pussy and you could see the thong underneath and she was worried because she didn't want me to appear like that in the photos. She was just as obsessed with Gloria's limping. She crouched down to even out the feathers on the wooden platform and repeated, "We're on television," passing us the flask of whiskey so we'd relax our bodies.

It was the only moment I felt my mother reinvigorated: when I was in front of an audience. Tears of emotion fell from her eyes, her face became illuminated. And not for nothing. We were fantastic. Super tan, and I had been on a diet since October, when I had learned Ricky was coming. Titina, the sales clerk at Chorus, had told me, and she was involved in organizing Carnaval. Four months of torture. Almost three weeks of complete fasting, but though just a bit emaciated, I was really happy. If I had died at that moment I would've been the happiest corpse in all Gualeguaychú. I couldn't believe that I didn't have to wear a girdle. Besides, a few days earlier, and only to reinforce the diet, I had found a box of laxatives and looked tiny. It's a pity I haven't seized advantage of the opportunity to continue taking care of myself. Because I'm such an anxiety-ridden person, a week after I stopped taking the pills, seeing him forever abandon my life, leaving me behind and discarded in Gualeguaychú, I gained it all back. And I hate being fat. But at least that day I was thinner than ever and he saw me. And besides, I did my own make-up on my nose so it looked like I'd had surgery done. Even mama, who is super demanding about make-up, congratulated me.

We took a photo with him in front of the municipal balcony. Us to each side wearing our big gaudy costumes and him between us with that marvelous smile just like the one on his posters. As he couldn't quite embrace us, he extended his arms; then he tilted his head a little towards Gloria. We looked like a little holy card of the crucifixion. He seemed so happy that I got all emotional. During one magic moment he pressed upon my shoulder with barely his fingertips and winked at me. I felt an electric charge coming from his arm and had to contain myself for the nineteen minutes I was near him because I thought I was going to have a heart attack. I was transported. Insensible, but quite sure I was going to see him again.

Gimpy and everything, Gloria danced better than I did. She had a better face, ass and attitude. She moved like never before when we reached Almafuerte Avenue and shone the whole night. But later the person talking with Ricky was me.

Ramón's brother worked at the disco and so got us two VIP tickets, but Gloria had a bit of a fever and was automatically left out.

The place was on fire, you couldn't fit a pin in there. Ricky showed up at 3:30 a.m. Two body guards in black t-shirts accompanied him to the VIP room. They dimmed the lights just for that. Complete darkness. I went to the bathroom to touch up my make-up, put on some perfume, and repeat "control" in front of the mirror with my hand out before me. And above all to wait, to suffer, to meditate for at least forty-five minutes until they dislodged all the girls who'd gone to besiege him asking for autographs. My goal was something more than that. I didn't want him to sign some piece of paper for me. I was ready to do anything to get something of his. My hands trembled, but the small super discrete ring I'd pierced my fingernail with looked fabulous on me.

All said and done, forty-five minutes later the VIP room at Gualeguaychú-Pamela was cleared and they weren't letting anyone in. I told Ramón I felt a little dizzy and asked him to please find me an aspirin, I wasn't going anywhere. When he disappeared from sight I headed straight for the VIP room. I took out my ticket and gave it to the bouncer. Ricky was sitting in a corner having a whiskey with Carlos María Reinoso, the host of a local cable show who'd just finished interviewing him. The two of them alone. I approached but the bodyguard in the black t-shirt wouldn't let me by. I tell him I was the baton twirler from the parade. I pull down the neckline of my blouse and show him my tits. He immediately goes "excuse me" and says he didn't recognize me because I look different, he looks them over and gives me a kiss. "Thanks," I reply and pass by. Just at that moment of complete ecstasy the disco version of "I Will Survive" begins to play. Ricky raises his head and looks at me but when I approach and am about to bend over and greet him, he drops his glass and starts gasping, as if he were suffocating, agitated and with a whistling in his chest that prevents him from reacting.

He turned purple. What happened next was complete confusion. I recall that Reinoso disappeared. The two bodyguards came over to ask what was wrong with him. Ricky still had his hand on his chest staring at me without saying anything, desperate to breathe.

I told them, "Don't worry, I'm a nurse. He's just had heat stroke, that's all," and I half-forced him to sit down. I undid three buttons on his shirt. He was in a cold sweat. "It's nothing," I said. "Just keep him calm." And looking him in the eyes, I said, "Breathe, sweetheart." I remember dying to smell his sweat. He was wearing a little medal of Our Lady of Lourdes. I couldn't believe we had the same one. Mine had been a gift from Nélida Doménico for my first communion. "We have to get him out of here," I told the bodyguards, because the poor thing was completely out of it. Then they picked him up and the four of us went out the rear exit into the patio. Everyone around was absolutely dying to know what was going on, but I ordered the bouncers to close the entrance to the outside area. "He needs to breathe," I told them, and we were the only ones to enter what would become the open air VIP lounge.

I massaged his chest for ten minutes trying to graze his nipples, to feel everything with my palms; and him with his eyes closed, breathing in life as if he were going to run out of air. Everything happened very quickly.

They brought him a glass bottle of mineral water. I gave him a few sips and wet his hair. He was wearing a killer cologne; I looked for a handkerchief I had in my purse, a white one with a big "E" embroidered on one side, and I dried him off completely, inch by inch, pressing my fingers on his forehead, his Adam's apple...I died of pleasure when my ring caught on his chest hairs. I didn't know what to do. I didn't want to yank them, and as I was in such a crazy state, what I did was rip off the piece of fingernail and discretely put it in my mouth with the ring and everything. I wished someone would have appeared with a camera to immortalize us in a portrait, but nobody showed up and I had to force my memory a thousand and one times to recall the moment second by second, so nothing would escape. My hands seemed designed to touch him my whole life. The white handkerchief was soaked. It gushed.

"What a scare!" was the first thing I said to him when he came to. By this time I was out of control and wasn't going to let him see me crying inconsolably. My heart was racing. I thought we were going to be together for eternity, then he looked at me like no one had ever done in my life, with the same eyes as the Jesus at the Church of the Eucharist. And he gave me a kiss. "Thanks, sweetheart," he said with a smile and then left.

I froze, the bottle of mineral water in one hand and the sopping handkerchief in the other. I felt closer to him than anybody in the world and at the same time on the edge of an abyss. The only thing that kept me from falling was the bottle of mineral water between the two of us with a quart of liquid. I held onto it, seeing how the disco was getting more and more crowded, until I found Ramón holding an aspirin. "Give it here," I told him, completely in tears. "I need it more than ever." And I felt the stream of water tracing its way through my stomach like a low-cal blood of Christ.

The next day I went over to Gloria's to tell her everything. She was in bed with a racing fever. I think she must have been sick with hatred, but when I finished telling her all the details she almost died. Of course I spiced it up a bit. I touched Ricky's legs and he hugged me until he couldn't take it anymore and cried at me not to let him die. "As badly upset as he was," I told her, "I could feel his dick was hard as ever." And later, in the end, when he'd already given me a farewell kiss, he promised we'd meet again so he could give me his latest CD. Green with envy, Gloria began straightening her sheets.

"What a beautiful box!" I said to change the subject, pointing at a carton lined with tissue paper that stuck out from under the nightstand, and when I bent down to touch it she screamed, "Don't go near it!" And that's when I understood how mad she really was. She furiously grabbed the box with both hands, gathering strength from I don't know where if she was so sick, picking it up fast as a weasel.

"What do you have there?" I asked her and a thousand things passed through my head, but I sat there mute, looking outside and remembering the times I'd had to go to the post office to see if my membership card in the Ricky Martin Fan Club had shown up. I never received it.

"It's my *secrétaire*," she shouted at me. And I responded, "Swear you don't have my card." And her, "I swear," kissing her finger, without thinking about it, putting the box under the covers. I had to bite my tongue because I hadn't let her see mine either. Then we hugged; the fight was over, period. Besides, swearing was sacred for us.

There was so much negative energy that I went into the kitchen to prepare us a cup of tea. The air was unbearable, smelling of the sick. Once in the patio, I went to the altar and crossed myself. The *equeco* seemed even more swollen next to Our Lady of Lourdes. The rain would clean it a little. I asked for a wish to be fulfilled and touched my little medal and I don't know why but I imagined he was doing the same thing.

I stayed there by the tea kettle waiting for the water. I smelled Ricky's scent everywhere; in my mind I went as far as seeing his desperate face, his wide open eyes, his dripping sweat. And I put my cold hand against his jaw; and the little ring getting entangled, and I looked at my hand, I felt I was going to choke and had to do something with my fingernail because it was horrible; then I screamed in fright. Gloria's mother touched me on the shoulder from behind, asking me to make her some tea; I was a bit unfocused, but nonetheless recounted to her all the details from the night at the disco. After the third round of *mate* she remained concentrated on one of my eyes, sipping on her straw. And I asked, "Something wrong with me, Hilda?" She lifted one of my eyelids and looked inside me and then did the same with the other. By now I was really intrigued. Her, nothing; she went to the refrigerator, took out an egg and drew a kind of border around me in the air and passed it over me until she stopped in the middle of my stomach. Me mute, holding onto the tea kettle. She went around my whole body again and then said to me in a very clear voice, "Girl, you're pregnant," like an ax blow. "No," I responded. And she insisted, "I'm telling you yes!" touching her chest. "The egg doesn't lie! What happened last night?"

"Everything," I responded, thinking of Ricky and the face he had when he saw me; in the smell of his sweat, in the little medal, but also remembering the fuck I had with Ramón. Like never before. I asked him to call me "sweetheart" and repeat it again and again, and him obeying because he was drunk. In and out with his face contorted like a madman. I was holding in my hands the bottle of water and the still damp handkerchief. I rubbed it all over my body. I looked at his head and I don't know why, but I wanted to split it open. But I put down the bottle and it finally ended.

I confirmed it three weeks later when I was late. I couldn't believe it. For a half hour I ranted at my panties. I pulled my hair. For a moment I wanted to go back in time and smash the bottle into Ramón's head like he deserved, to see if he had finally learned to control himself.

I retched. I plopped down everywhere and once even fell down the stairs. It's that I had bought myself some jeans two sizes too small and turned pale because of how bad I was feeling. I went to get the pregnancy test in really bad shape and with a huge bruise on my belly. Seeing the hematoma, the doctor asked me if I'd been beaten. I told him yes and he offered to go with me to the police station to file a complaint. What a dear, but I told him it wasn't worth the trouble, and took out the white handkerchief with the "E" that I thought I'd never wash again and didn't stop crying until it was soaked. I'd given up all hope.

I returned home pressing the damp "E" to my heart. I hated Ramón with all my soul. "Son of a bitch," I screamed at him a million times, taking refuge in Ricky's eyes when he desperately looked at me in the discotheque courtyard. I even felt like having a cigarette, anti-smoker that I am.

Mama reacted to the news the way she reacted to everything, like a mummy. Nothing new. She was holding a glass of whiskey and slurred her words for a couple of steps. Benito took advantage of her being distracted to escape; we heard the car taking off while the two of us lost ourselves, she in her pain and me with Ramón's child confirmed inside the envelope.

As soon as I mentioned abortion she began to scream, as if she had been waiting. "Please, enough crimes in this house," she said to me, making a scene which had it been broadcast on the air would have been moving. Her voice cracked. Tears streaming down her face, real snot running from her nose. "Mama, I can't have Ramón's child," I told her. "He's a nobody. I want to have a baby with Ricky Martin and for the last month I've been trying to achieve just that. This close," I repeated, holding two fingers apart to show how close I had come to having him inside me. "I think you and Ricky Martin would be good together," she suddenly said to me, calmer, her eyes filled with tears. She looked like a tiny little creature.

The television was turned off. On the screen you could see our opaque reflections, as if we'd been drained of all brightness and contrast. It had been a long, long time since we'd been like this. Embracing, crying without fighting, without Benito coming between us, like when we used to fall asleep in front of the television even when the programming was off because we didn't like to be alone in the dark. "Mosquito race," she used to say, the two of us dazed by the little dots of light on the screen and the sound like a storm the transmission made.

Mama fell asleep with her head on my shoulder. I had to undo my pants because I couldn't take the pain anymore. I was afraid I was going to faint. There was a new bottle of nail polish on the side table; I grabbed it and up close the color looked horrible. It didn't go with anything. Beside it mama's pack of L&M Lights almost full, a cigarette sticking half out. I stretched out two fingers but couldn't reach it because I had her whole weight falling on top of me and didn't want to wake her. Her hair smelled like cigarettes.

Using the bottle of nail polish, I finally managed to reach the pack. I was really worked up. I put one in my mouth, my lips trembling. I took a deep drag and ended up in a scary coughing fit and mama running to the kitchen to get me a glass of water and a Mydol, asking if I wanted a cup of tea. "No, forget it," I said to her. "Teach me how to smoke," and she sat down beside me. She offered me a cigarette from the pack and began looking on the table for the lighter, which I had; then, because I was shaking, I raised both hands well out before me, as if I were praying, and lit it.

Three days later I aborted, naturally.

10

At Chakira I ran into the whole Ricky Martin Fan Club. I went all dressed in black. Lupe, Marisa Mellman and her brother, the Dellors twins, ugly as ever, and a group of sick things better not described. I couldn't believe how strong Mellman's brother Patricio was; it seemed strange him talking with someone because he was always alone, into his own things, quiet, with enormous arms from lifting weights so much. I thought he was really hot. He was the only person who made me forget about Ricky for a moment. I went up to greet him, and after the hi, how you doing, I put a hand on his waist. He had perfectly defined obliques and one of my fingers rested just on the line made in the middle of the muscles. "I'm all right," he answered to my face, making me feel a bit uncomfortable for a second while he went on talking with the other kid who had even a stronger build. I immediately took my hand away, but I still waited anxiously for the moment they would let me break into the conversation.

They didn't even look my way again, ignoring me. "Shitty queers," I thought, remembering the night we had slept over at the Mellmans' house after a recital.

I was happy to get to sleep in the same bed with Patricio, it was killer. At first I breathed into his shoulders, into the nape of his neck. Him, nothing. I rested my chin on his shoulder and gave him a kiss, because after a concert I was always horny; then pretending I was asleep I embraced him and pressed myself against him and also sleeping he managed to move me off himself very gently. Divine, but I don't think he got a hard on and I couldn't sleep at all with his breath and his legs brushing against me all night. And despite Marisa always denying it, between us we used to gossip that although it wasn't obvious, Patricio was kind of gay; if not, then what should have happened between us would have happened. Another disillusion. Different chapter.

We sat at the bar and ordered rum *caipiriñas*. There was a tequila promotion and each bottle had a sticker with Ricky's face on it. I was dying to have them all, but they were only giving away one per person. Nothing. Luckily Lupe chatted up the guy at the bar, who ended up giving us two of each of the little bottles. I kept one for a more important occasion, but the girls emptied theirs out completely in their drinks. We were out of control and getting crazy. I remembered that at home I'd only had one little container of flan, two or three crackers and nothing else, and after drinking alcohol I'm always attacked by hunger and I like to have something in reserve because it calms me down. I'd have to stop at some newsstand to get a couple macaroons or some candy.

By the time Ricky arrived each of us had already downed three drinks. He looked fabulous, wearing a white shirt with buttoned cuffs, and more radiant than ever. It looked like he was being carried along by his bodyguards.

A ton of make-up. Irma had recounted to me how as he had bad skin, she covered it with a quarter-inch layer of foundation and they lit the lights to 4000 volts. "That's why he sweats so much during his show, girl, because of that," she told me. "It's pure make-up, like you." At that instant I see myself standing behind the stage in the middle of a concert, waiting with a towel ready to dry him off, having cancelled two interviews for him, one on CNN and the other on E!Entertainment, because he looked tired, and he thanks me, caressing my cheek, and I give him a touch of concealer and transparency powder because I want to take care of his image all by myself and no one else is going to touch him. And everybody else dying of envy asking who I am, and him at the press conference after the show relating the moment he met me, the story about how I saved his life at the disco in Gualeguaychú, and three women journalists in the front row wipe their tears all at the same time, and one of them raises both hands to ask an urgent question and I'm standing next to Ricky, a little bit behind him, ultra discrete, wearing a plain white t-shirt, tight jeans, without a sole roll of fat because I'd just had liposuction even to my hands, and plastic surgery on the nose is out and make-up like mine is the absolute hypermax, and in a nice way I ask with an almost Durán-like tone of voice that the photographers please not shoot their flashbulbs in my face because it bothers me and with one hand I cover my face and once again right in my eyes, I point at the journalist, furious, and then another flash. And all of a sudden I'm brought back to reality.

I landed super dizzy and alone at the bar. Luckily. Since I started working in television I preferred not being seen with the girls. The flashes were real, because Ricky had just crossed through the middle of the disco with a couple of bodyguards. I couldn't stand up. "María" was playing and I had to close my legs from the emotion. I headed toward the bathroom the best I could. The place was spinning around me.

When I saw myself clearly in the mirror I almost had a heart attack. I was a wretch and had nothing in my purse to rescue me. I took off my shoes; there were three enormous floor-to-ceiling mirrors placed in such a way I could see all of myself, and I took advantage to adjust my nylons in back. If I looked a bit to the side I could see my body multiplied a thousand times, each reflection becoming smaller and smaller until ending in a little dot of light. I touched my chest and felt my sweaty palms. Just then some girl came in and I asked her if she had some powder. And her in a thick voice with a heavy Spanish accent, "No, but I have something that'll get you in the right mood." She looked at me from head to toe. "You're going to have a very special night," she said. "What sign are you?" And me, "Pisces." Then she took out a little bottle that looked like a perfume flask. She sat there with her eyes closed, contracting the muscles in her face, and pressed two fingers on her nose as if she'd burned herself. "Inhale." And me obedient because she'd taken on a much better mien, but I had to move my nose away because of how strong it was, like ammonia. "No, inhale as deeply as you can," she said. Then copying her I took a big snort and squeezed my nose with two fingers. And her, "It's like you see little stars, no?" and although nothing like that I said yes because I felt like I was in the clouds. I seemed to hear the music at full blast and I couldn't believe what had happened to my face. I looked divine and the chick hugged me from behind and with one hand lifted my chin so I'd look at myself in the mirror. Then with her other hand she cupped my tits and grabbing them told me she was going to devour them bite by bite. Nothing less. I gave her an elbow and despite the disgust the idea gave me I couldn't stop laughing.

Nor could I stop dancing. I felt like La Bomba Tucumana and climbed up on a speaker with two other girls who were out of control until I slipped and my blouse accidentally opened, my bra came undone and sprawled on the ground one of my tits was showing to the perverts gathered around me. The face of the girl from the bathroom in the front row.

I felt like nothing was going to hold me back; sprawled there on the floor I imagined I was the sexiest thing that mob of imbeciles had seen in years. I gathered my strength and headed for the VIP area with such great luck that just at that moment the bouncers were tossing some girl who'd passed out. I took advantage of the hysterics to slip in and didn't stop until I got to the bar. The music seemed louder to me on that side, the people more beautiful, the atmosphere different. And they put on some instrumental, kind of like the theme song from "Star Wars," and in the background a siren accompanied by the sound of thunder that gave it enormous impact. The lights were spinning round and round, and in the middle of it all...a miracle.

Ricky, like an apparition, with his back turned dancing alone in front of me; a light fell right on him that drew a kind of fluorescent border around him. The crystal balls in the ceiling cast multi-colored butterflies all over the floor. Fabulous.

I walked in a straight line, this I remember perfectly, and when he turned around, following the advice of Nélida Doménico, I surprised him. "Whoa," he said.

"We're moving kind of fast!" He was talking to me. And all excited I replied, "Don't you believe it. I've been thinking about this for three years and just got the courage to do it right now." And I went up and said in his ear, "The thing is, I want to have your baby." I couldn't believe what was happening to me. His white teeth leapt out from the black light falling on him. It seemed everybody had fallen silent and the music had stopped so they could hear the moment I pronounced that famous phrase of Grecia Colmenares in "Topaz," and I imagined him throwing me on the floor and making the child with me right there, with all his passion and the people spinning around us. Then he replied, breaking the magic of the moment, "And I want to have a baby with Princess Di," taking my hand from him with a kindness that made me tremble.

The smiling face of the princess was branded upon me. "A baby with Princess Di, Princess Di..." echoed in my head, and I imagined her in her little black corduroy hat entering the Sheraton. That's all I remember and the voice of Esperanza Gracia shouting at me a change of life and environment and Ricky's face going off with his free-flowing hair covered with butterflies from the dance floor and after that the images get blurry, the conversations, the music, everything; as if I'd fallen into a time tunnel, but instead of the original one with red and green circles from the show appeared the diamonds from the shoe box Gloria had brought home, a very intense lilac and orange; with a lost gaze and the sensation of being one of those spirits from the special they showed on Channel 13, "Perception After Death." The body abandoned, distant; but worst of all I don't remember anything. And once again nothing is nothing. And I have to trust in Gloria's version, which is certainly exaggerated. Humiliating. It was like having missed the best part of the show.

When I came to I was luckily at home. In my panties and bra. Gloria, nestled at the foot of my bed, was channel surfing and staring at the TV: she looked like the little girl in "Poltergeist." It smelled like a barn. In my head exploded the sequence of images from the day before. Ultraconfused. I couldn't think. There was a mountain of *TV Guide*s on the floor all scattered about, the scissors opened wide and the bottle of black nail polish off to the side. My head spinning a thousand miles per hour. I thought I must have been in a very serious state. So much so that Gloria hadn't even started to straighten up yet.

She recounted to me how at noon I'd become really crazy. Bursting out laughing and then a little later all a fury and then laughing again. She told me that just when she arrived the television was reporting news about Angélica Durán's accident. A camera at the Apart Hotel had filmed the fatal moment and they showed a flash of the bottom of the elevator with an image of her face and her elbows pinned to the springs at the depths of the shaft. It was like they had put her into a giant blender because after she fell the trump card was that the elevator came down on top of her and she didn't have time to do anything. The firemen had to take it apart to rescue her remains incrusted at the bottom of the shaft.

You see everything on the film. The door opened by itself but the elevator wasn't there and looking spaced out first she took a step forward, puts down a heel and falls forward with all her momentum and an uncharacteristic grace, like she's about to enter some cognac ad in *Vogue*.

You can even hear her screams and see how the elevator continues down and then goes free, causing the catastrophe. Gloria was speechless and tried to explain things with her hands. She told me what happened next was that I remained passed out like I was in a coma and slept at least nine hours straight, that she gave me a revitalizing massage but I wouldn't come to. At one moment she felt so desperate she called Damian, her friend the masseur, so he'd come over and see if I was all right. He calmed her way down and advised her to let me sleep. With a disapproving tone I said, "He was here?" because I didn't like him at all. Gloria knew that perfectly but ignored my comment. And then that evening I woke up at 10 with a face that frightened her and went to the bathroom in a trance, my eyes bulging out of my head. I took out my make-up and began paging through the last three *TV Guide*s, one by one, looking for a photo. She smelled something strange and called Lupe.

Her sister answered, and she was really worried, too, because Lupe was as out of it as I was. She had tried to jump out the window with a poster of Ricky wrapped around herself. They came to the conclusion we'd had something put in our drinks. And sure it was Marisa Mellman, who was already famous for slipping things into the drinks of people she wanted to get rid of, just like her father and the whole branch of the family who were pharmacists. They concluded that cow had for sure put something in our drinks.

Gloria hung up and took care of me the whole time. She didn't leave for one minute. She asked me what I was looking for and I said, "A photo of Princess Di." I was so frantic that she also began looking for the damned picture and found it first and I yanked it from her hands and then put it up with a thumbtack in the middle of the cork-board. Pointing at the photo, I asked, "What might that little princess be doing?" And I answered myself, "That one I don't know, but this one," sticking a finger in the middle of my chest, "is going to do her nails." And I began to paint them black. While I was doing that I confessed to her without holding back a word that I was the killer of my sister, my first child, Parmessano and Durán. And that it was Nélida Doménico who'd pushed me to go for Ricky, and had even promised she'd get me his cell phone number through a contact she had. "No man, no matter how famous he is," she had told me, "can resist a nice Argentine girl." And I hinted to Gloria about my short term plans for the princess. "Pray for her," I asked, "because she doesn't have much time to live."

She asked me innocently, "And you think that's going to work for you long-distance like the Internet?" And at that moment I raised my hand and gave the last little brush to my thumb. And the other in front of me looking and looking without knowing what to do. "What do you think?" I said to her, raising my voice, indignant, without seeing her face because I had one eye closed and my finger covered her features. And I finished my nails in silence. They looked fantastic painted black.

We watched television with the magazine torn between the two of us, full of scissor cuts, and during a commercial I say, "Come here," and she follows me. I scream at her, "Don't drag your feet! I have a headache," and Gloria does everything she can to obey me as she follows me down the hall. I begin to count my steps in a low voice while I dry my nails waving my hands in the air. We go into my room, I grab the Polaroid and hand it to her. I turn off the lights and turn on a nightlight, get all mysterious and then ask her, "What day is today?" "August 30," she says. And me, "What time is it in Europe?" And she answers, "3:30 a.m. on the 31st," because she knows what time it is in every country Ricky travels to: Puerto Rico, the U.S., anyplace he might be she's able to follow him with her thoughts. I can, too.

I finish counting thirteen steps right in front of the cork-board. "Frame it well and remember the time," I say to her while I put a hand on the portrait of Princess Di and with one pull rip it in half. Gloria was praying. It was 3:33 a.m., a Saturday dawn in Europe, and you could cut the air in my room with a knife. Not for nothing. Nobody in the history of humanity had killed two famous people in just twenty-four hours. Nobody except me, of course. And without leaving my house. Invading everything, the flash from the camera made me close my eyes.

11

Gloria turned paler than a ghost. She was finishing telling me all about how my head had suffered a disconnection of memory and both of us were unplugged. She'd been changing channels for more than an hour, like a zombie, I felt like I was about to vomit and when I couldn't take it any more I screamed at her, "Keep still!" because everything bugged me. Then we stayed on the news channel and five seconds later came the first report about the princess.

Although foreseeable, the news hit us like a bucket of water in the face. "Princess Di has been killed," said a red and white banner at the same time the newscaster announced it like a goal in a soccer game. "They killed her," said Gloria in a quiet voice, while she crossed herself.

I looked her straight in the eyes and said, "Don't even think about saying a word about what happened. To anyone, because you're just as guilty as I am. We're accomplices," I remarked to her.

"I didn't do anything," she said on the verge of tears.

"You did nothing to stop it," I said.

The car looked like a wrecked ball, a heap of metal, and there were a lot of cops there. They had taken the princess to the hospital with her little injured vegetarian face. They recounted how she was in a coma four hours before she died; just like me, who did everything without remembering anything, not even my name. Without knowing what Ricky did when he took my hand away from there, which is when I think I lost consciousness. I cursed the girl in the bathroom and Marisa Mellman and Lupe; Mellman's brother, too, for being a faggot, although he had the nicest legs in the discotheque. I remembered Ricky's face saying he wanted to have a baby with Princess Di and automatically he changed into her and her teeth shone from the black light that covered her whole body. I felt more full of life than ever. So strong that I thought something of the princess had been transmitted to me. Thinner, taller and with a nose full of personality. I grabbed my wrists; my hands were cold.

Gloria sat there stiff on the sofa, and when I managed to gather my strength I called Nélida Doménico. "I have something for you," she said to me. I needed that: someone who gave me a push, not a statue. I stood up straight; I had to get used to that position. A hunched back, in addition to fucking up your spine, doesn't look very good on television. "You have to look at the cameras as if someone were pulling on your head from behind with a little string," I'd heard the puppet host of a TV talk show once say and I repeated it to my colleagues at the station.

It was Nélida who advised me to go see Ricky that very day, saying I had to think of myself first and the rest would fall into place. She understood my situation very well because she was the lover of a famous actor I can't name; and despite them having a child, she kept the relation secret while in public he maintained his other family. But as she said, "Every month *ca-ching, ca-ching*," and she rustled little pieces of paper as if they were bills. "And if not," she said to me getting all serious, "you send him to straighten it out with a judge. There's no fucking around with DNA, girl." I was about to burst into tears. I asked her for a couple phone numbers. One was Ricky's cell and the other a gynecologist, a friend of hers who takes care of everybody in show business. She told me to remind him I was like a daughter to her and moreover an extra on "The Condemned." "I'm sure he'll give you a special price," and then she commented, "And what about Angélica!" And me, "Please, don't talk to me about that now because I'm feeling very sensitive, a complete wreck," and I told her that the day before I'd been talking to her in the station's parking garage. "So beautiful," I said, "so full of life. She looked divine." And Nélida, "I heard she was doing drugs." "Me, too, but even so I thought she was great," I lied. "What a loss for Argentine television," she lamented, and we sat there another thirty minutes talking about the global misfortune caused by the other disaster, that of Princess Di. Nélida compared her to a shooting star, and I could only reply she always had the right words for everything.

"Dr. Carlos Castillo, artificial insemination," I wrote down on the cover of the latest *TV Guide*, and the telephone number below it. I felt like the happiest person on earth. I raised my arms in a victory sign to Gloria. Like Wonder Woman, joining my fists and biting my lower lip. "We're unbeatable," I said to her. And I took the phone to my room so I could talk more privately.

Ricky answered himself. I didn't know what to say to him. I had put on my robe and lots of perfume, but still felt naked. I explained we'd been together the night before and that I'd had him all to myself until he put Princess Di in the middle of everything. "And let me be clear that I only killed her to show you what I'm capable of doing just to sleep with you," I told him. I wanted to sound experienced and I felt like the strongest woman alive.

At first a saint. He listened to me in silence. But when I finished he screamed at me I was crazy and if this were a joke it was in the worst taste.

"Don't hang up," I begged him on my knees beside my bed. "I don't want to do you any harm," but he didn't listen to me. I was shattered, this was the second occasion in less than forty-eight hours they'd shouted the same thing in my face. Why me?! Why did he of all people have to say it?! Coming from a viper like Durán it was no big deal, but Ricky! 70% of my life devoted to him and this is how he pays me back? I felt cheated, persecuted, cornered. I could feel the scorn in my broken heart, and I imagined the word CRAZY in capital letters blinking in the middle of the page in *TV Guide*. I could see a picture of me and Durán in the garage, because I was sure there was a camera filming everything and on the other page the Polaroid where I'm ripping apart the photo of Lady Di with my eyes closed. I was about to put on a song by Luis Miguel, but I was sorry the moment I thought it, and I asked his forgiveness, looking him in the eyes of his poster.

Everything seemed black. I needed something to pick me up. I opened my purse and took out the little promotional bottle of tequila, drinking it down in one gulp. I tried again, looking at his little face on the sticker of the bottle. I pushed "redial," grabbed my silk scarf and felt a sword of fire going from my throat to my stomach, following the same path as my anguish and desolation. I looked at myself in the mirror. I was completely in tears.

This time I went straight to the point. I disguised my voice; I felt like Angélica Durán in "The Condemned," and told him in the hottest tone I could, "Hi, Ricky, my name is Esperanza Hóberal and if you don't sleep with me I'm going to kill you." He hung up. I took a deep breath and counted to ten. I couldn't hold back my weeping.

I didn't want to get carried away by impulse. I had to calculate well. I could tell it wasn't going to be so easy, and for that reason I tried to keep calm. Mama's face appeared to me saying, "Con-trol," while she lowered her raised hand down to her chin. I put on his latest CD and "I Loved You" began playing at full volume. I stood in front of the mirror. I had to be careful not to overdo it with the poster of Ricky. He looked so beautiful in that photo. So close and so mine. I gave him three little pecks and secured it to the corkboard with nine tacks. It was an incredible poster, double-size, that had come in a special issue of *TV Guide* dedicated to him. A photo where he's just coming out of the pool, a towel in hand and his legs well defined. Wet and looking at the camera out of the corner of his eye, barely smiling as if they'd caught him by surprise. The towel covers almost his entire black bikini, and if you try hard it looks like he's naked. It's a photo they took in Miami because in Argentina, he once confessed on the radio, he had never worn a bikini.

Outside the door, Gloria asked me what I was doing and I asked her to please leave me alone.

"Don't do anything to him," she begged anxiously.

"Of course not!" I shouted at her, approaching and holding the phone. "Of course not," and I pounded on the door with my hand and heard the shocked scream from the other side. "Go away," I told her and she didn't say anything more.

When the poster was unrolled flat and Ricky facing me and making fun of me with his smile, I made two marks on it in the form of an X. I took a deep breath and stuck my finger in his ankle until I felt the cork at the base of my fingernail. At that moment, coming out of the bathroom with a divine orange towel wrapped around himself and just about to step down into the sunken living room, he tripped on the stair and lay sprawled on the floor with a twisted ankle, crying in pain. I, too, was suffering. I imagined him crouched over and grabbing his leg, perhaps remembering me for the first time. I got all excited.

I gave him three minutes to recover, tied the silk scarf around my right wrist and called back. I told him, "I don't want to hurt you but now you see what I'm forced to do if you don't listen to me." And I seized the opportunity to also tell him about Angélica Durán so he would show me a bit more respect. Him, nothing.

"Does it hurt?" I asked. Silence. "Sweetheart, does it hurt?" I insisted. And then him, divine, "A bit," and like a good intuitive Capricorn this time he listened to me. "I'm incapable of hurting anybody, especially someone like you." "I'm going to turn you in," he said. And me, "I won't give you time," and I swear to God this time it wasn't my nail but just a bit of pressure with my fingertip and then I heard a scream from the other end of the line. "I don't want to hurt you," I repeated. "I want a car to come by for me in half an hour," and there my voice cracked but I gave him the address, and before hanging up I threatened him, assuring that if in thirty-one minutes there wasn't someone at the door of my house, the whole world would always remember me. I hung up. When I came out Gloria was sitting in the hallway listening, hugging her *equeco* in the total darkness.

"Mariquita Valenzuela used to say that," the bitch told me. "How do you know?" I asked, upset because I hated her listening in on my conversations. "She used to be my favorite," she said, and without paying any more attention I gave her Dr. Castillo's phone number so she could make an urgent appointment for me. "They're coming to get me soon," I told her. "I have to take a shower." I felt like a big star.

On TV they were saying that Diana's car had smashed into column #13 and you could see perfectly the two skid marks from the Mercedes. One of the witnesses talked about a giant flash, like he'd seen an explosion. They showed the revolving door at the Hotel Ritz in Paris, and inside you could see the princess taking the last spin of her life and going down the corridor without looking at the security camera that focused on her from above.

The telephone rang and my heart stopped. When I answered they hung up. Gloria and I sat there looking at each other. Ten seconds later it rang again and she said, "Let me get it," super mysterious, hurrying to the phone so I wouldn't pick up. And to my surprise she began talking as if nothing had happened and she turned her back to me because it was the fat masseur. I didn't like Gloria's attitude and that tub of lard stuck in my throat more and more, but luckily I had something important to do and I went up to remind her not to forget my appointment with Dr. Castillo.

I turned on the shower and looked at myself in the mirror. I needed a total makeover. I had terrible dark circles under my eyes and my hair looked like a mop. It would have been great to go to the salon and at the same time shave my legs, because the hair made me a bit warm. And then appeared to me mama's face on the day I left Gualeguaychú, with her half-dry hair standing on end from the static electricity; my wooden butterfly broken in half; Benito coming into my room; the sound of the hairdryer getting louder and then mama's face appearing in the door and her hand stretching out to grab my hair. I had to leave the bathroom for a minute because I had the feeling something strange was happening. My head began to ache. Gloria with her back to me in the living room was waving the little piece of paper with Dr. Castillo's telephone number as if she were drying it in the air and I heard her saying, "Satan! The spell is cast," and just then she turned around and looked at me. I crossed myself; I had no desire to invoke anything strange and much less on that day.

It was horrible. My mother forced me down the steps of the house screaming, "May God forgive you, because I can't!" I closed my eyes and tried to scare her from my thoughts, remembering the music they used to play in the Church of the Eucharist to chase away the devil. There was no point; I felt like crying. And very scared. I could see mama climbing up the steps of the Academy De Biasio dressed all in black with the little photo of me and my sister that appeared in *Real Life Cases*. Lost in herself. Then, desperate to reinforce the effect and drive her completely away, I turned the stereo on full blast and everything was taken care of.

Gloria closed the living room door with a kick and even that made me feel bad. My jaw trembled, I felt more sensitive than ever. Raw emotion.

12

Just as expected, at 5 p.m. on the dot a dark guy in a long-sleeved black shirt rang the doorbell of my apartment. I wasn't ready and he had to wait more than twenty minutes for me. My clothing options included two winter outfits, four summer, and a very daring one with a low neckline and slit skirt, but in the end I decided on something simpler. It was one of the most difficult decisions of my life.

I was wearing a pound of foundation and I glowed. I'd painted my lips with a black pencil brush that didn't run so much, but beneath it was a very subtle lilac to give it light. My eyes almond-shaped, like Durán on "The Condemned." My nose, ultra made up. Placed in the ensemble of the face, it looked like a work of art.

The guy led me to a black Mercedes with tinted windows that made my heart race, while Gloria's gaze followed me from the balcony. She waved goodbye like I was a queen. Before going down I asked her, "What are you going to do?" I was worried about her. She seemed tense and had dark circles under her eyes.

"Pray," she replied and hugged me with all her might, like we hadn't held each other in a while. I loved Gloria a lot, but at that moment I felt like we were blood sisters and at such a delicate stage of my life she was there for me, strong as iron. "Enough, I'm going to cry and I can't," I told her, opening my eyes wide and pressing my fingers to their sides to hold back the tears. I looked at myself in the mirror in a typical gesture of Angélica. "You look fantastic," Gloria said, adjusting the wide-brimmed hat she'd lent me, which went well with the oiled braid that fell to my waist. The extension was a loan from Irma, the station's make-up artist, that Graciela Alfano used to wear. Everyone had done their little part and I was going completely given over to my meeting with Ricky.

I was praying the heat was on in the Mercedes because in the thirty feet I had to walk from the entrance of the building I'd almost frozen. As well I wanted to be lightly dressed and just in case brought along a divine silk scarf that looked killer on me, and should the case arise, in two minutes I'd be ready and waiting. The big dark guy opened the door for me and we headed towards Palermo, turning down Independence Avenue in an ideal temperature. He looked at me in the mirror, not taking his eyes off my tits the whole way.

"How is he?" I asked.

"How is he what?" the beast answered.

"His ankle," I said impatiently.

"He's lying down with a bag of ice on it," he said, not saying any more about the matter. I frowned just in case, relieved he didn't suspect anything. I killed time looking at my gorgeous fall jacket, lilac with pleats on each side that made me look thin. The skirt: short and black. Nylons, of course. Five-inch heels. Fantastic. Lighter eyeshadow to illuminate my eyes. The concealer had delineated my features, giving them an upswept air, although it couldn't rid me of my worried look. Nor could I stop looking at myself in a little mirror that I carried in my coin purse, very fitting for this type of situation that requires discretion: a little rectangle where my mouth barely fit, nothing more. Perfect.

"It looks like it's going to start coming down anytime," the guy said at a stoplight, looking out the window at the sky. And me, "It's certainly going to rain, no?" And him, "The rains are coming but they're late." "Really?" I answered, and at that moment came to mind the image of my sister telling my mother through Hilda De Biasio, in the little room of the dead, step by step about the explosion in our house, and mama super attentive to every detail: when my sister states my name, when she repeats it, when she touches her chest and begins to cry. I forced myself to close my eyes and not think anymore, because I sensed at any moment we were going to arrive and I had to be together. The guy handed me a tissue to dry my eyes. I held it up to them and absorbed the tears without out a drop of mascara running. A complete professional. To change the topic he said, "Let's tune in the weather forecast," but there wasn't time.

We arrived right at that moment. My face livened up. The guy pressed a remote control and the door opened wide. The corner of Niceto Vega and Bonpland. From outside it didn't look like much at all, but inside it knocked me dead. Stunning. The garage door closed by itself. I saw little red dots of light every six feet and imagined they were cameras. I got out of the car and stood up straight, sure he must be someplace observing me on the monitors. Or perhaps the FBI was inside, gathering evidence to lock me up; mama would probably testify against me and they'd send me to jail. Better that not be the case because then they'd know who they were dealing with. And that wasn't a threat, it was a promise. I couldn't remember on what soap opera I'd hear that phrase. I stared at one of the little red lights so in case they were looking at me they'd understand the message. I took care not to raise my shoulders too much in order to look natural. The guy let me by and we climbed the stairs.

There was a fabulous mirror. I looked at myself from head to toe. Impeccable. My wrap playing off the walls, and to the side a long table full of photos and papers. I held myself back from running over and looking through everything. And I only did so because there was also a door covered in green vinyl upholstered with colorful tacks. I was paralyzed. It was the same one that used to appear in my dreams in Gualeguaychú when I was a little girl. Identical. As if out of the movie "Days of Illusion." I crossed my fingers; I remember that in my dream the door also opened automatically, and flying in upon my giant orange butterfly I was dragged towards the abyss down an unending precipice and the walls of the void I fell through were transformed into a trembling heart of flesh and blood, with muscle fibers and everything, and me sinking into its precipice.

I practiced making my mouth sexy. A natural face, but as if biting my canines. My hands calm and the fingers a bit raised. The guy invited me to go in. My legs were trembling. My heart raced a thousand miles an hour. There was bland background music, like something provided by the Sheraton. Classical. There was no television, no monitors, no FBI. I relaxed. He was at the back of the room lying on a bed, a white terry cloth robe wrapped around him. I approached. He had his right leg resting upon a big pillow and on top of it an ultramodern inflatable bag of ice in a loud turquoise. Obviously imported.

"Alone at last," I said to him, and smiled to hide my nervousness.

I sat on the edge of the bed. At the foot, with my legs stretched out before me like the hands of the clock marking 5:40. I felt as naked and vulnerable as he did. I was dying of love. I asked him if it hurt; he nodded. It was impossible to take my eyes from his package, as if it were a magnet. He had fabulous legs. I touched him with my hand to see his reaction. Him divine, not a peep.

"I understand this isn't my best moment," I said, showing him the photo of us taken in front of the Gualeguaychú city hall. With our big ugly feathered costumes. "I'm not going to force you to do anything." Him mute. I thought, "He's either in shock or drugged." I spread his legs apart. I didn't want to force the situation, but the way things were going nothing was going to happen; I was doing all I could, and him with a face full of panic.

I had to wait quite a while until it got the way it was supposed to get. Nor did the music help, but I gave it my best and after a while we started getting along better. More relaxed, I asked him why he had treated me so badly at the Sheraton and then he said, "I know who you are," and his face changed, it was like falling in love again because moreover he asked me to forgive him. I said, "It doesn't matter anymore." And although I was crying, I felt like the happiest person on earth.

Then I stood up and asked him to please play the ninth song on the CD *Ricky Martin* and I performed the entire video of "You'll Be Back" because I knew it by heart. First I spun around a stool. I knelt on the edge just like the girl in it, who did that super well, with her hair in her face, and then me playing with my braid and later the chorus part with the dance and everything, which I did better than ever, and he even began to sing softly while I finished the number, making a superhuman effort so that my foundation and eye shadow didn't become a complete mess.

I opened my purse, took out the white handkerchief and a little container of caramel that Gloria had stolen by the thousands from the Sheraton. I spread it all over his thing and used the little mirror to look at myself, since there were no cameras to record the moment.

I was floating, but when he grabbed my head with both hands I melted with tenderness. "Please, if you're going to come I'd love to ask you something," I said while I interrupted my task for a moment. Besides I was choking. He nodded, delivering himself over to me.

"Sing me 'I Loved You,'" I said. "I promise you it's the last thing I ask."

"But then you're not…" he responded, the poor little saint, looking at his dick and shrugging his shoulders. I was ready to eat him up. And he brightened, remembering that song was on the same CD, and pressed number four on the remote control, which was just killer.

He came a moment later, arching his back a little and holding onto my head with his two hands, the remote control tangled in my braid. And to think at first I was scared he was never going to get a hard on. With the shock, with the pain in his ankle, with the nerves, with reason.

I was thrilled. I went into the bathroom and spit everything in my mouth into the little tequila bottle I had brought along just for that reason. I wiped my lips with the white handkerchief. He smiled at me from the sticker. I was also carrying his glass bottle from Gualeguaychú and filled it with tap water.

Pure happiness. I swear on my mother that before I left he hugged me. And in the background was playing "La Bomba." I didn't know what to say, I asked him if it was a new song, and he said yes, that it was his latest demo, and me, "Please don't move," and he hobbled over to the stereo on one foot and gave it to me.

The weather was horrible. On the way back the whole scene appeared to me like a movie that began with Gloria's embrace at the apartment door and ended with me going down the steps, crying, my jacket buttoned up and holding the bottles and him at the top of the stairs with his robe open, his dick hanging down and a face of respect that only results from the shock of rape, and finally the words "The End" in red off to one side.

I swore by mama, by Gloria and by Nélida Doménico that I was never going to go crazy again. Ricky's son, while I was alive, was going to have a normal mother like everybody else. And I imagined that when everything was over and I could relate what I'd had to do to be happy, Mirta would invite me on her show and help everyone learn the truth. And then mama appears in my thoughts and I can't help it no matter how much I try and she screams at me, "Mirta doesn't invite killers!" and she holds the "s" like a serpent. I answer her, "If that murderer Yiya Murana was on, she'll certainly invite me." And I recalled what Zulema Yoma had once said while having lunch with Mirta, that in life if we don't have hope, we're dead. I wanted to demonstrate that to the entire world, and I asked the driver to stop at the first pay phone. I wanted to make an urgent call. I had to pour my heart out.

The wind had really picked but it didn't bother me because I felt like I was in heaven. After making my urgent call, I dialed mama's telephone in Gualeguaychú. When she answered, I hung up. Lately I had been doing that all the time. I only wanted to hear her voice.

I couldn't believe it. Fifty feet from the phone booth I saw an immense sign saying "Doll Clinic" and went up to the shop window in a kind of daze. On one side were all the repaired dolls and on the other all the loose pieces they sold for pennies a piece. I thought about Jocelyn, my dark-skinned Barbie, calculating the good it would do us to bring her by the clinic, and was just about to memorize the phone number when I remembered I had it written down in my notebook of sayings, and at that moment the guy honked the horn. The storm was about to let loose.

I ran to the car trying not to let the first drops get me wet. "Just in time," he said. "Now it's coming down." And we sped off.

13

The swarthy guy driving dropped me off at my door as if I were a princess. He had to park on the sidewalk because the storm was really coming down. Every two seconds a bolt of lightening flashed and he, ever the gentleman, tried to make with his body a tunnel to protect me, while the door and umbrella were flying all over. We ended up soaking wet anyways; him with the shirt sticking to his body like a stud, and then three seconds later he disappeared at full speed like a madman, spraying water from the sides of the car.

I felt ground down by fatigue. The first thing I did was take off my shoes in the foyer; a deep, full breath, like Gloria recommended, to calm down and just then I realized there was no light anywhere in the building. A nightmare. Nine flights of steps: deadly. You couldn't see anything and no light always puts me in a bad mood. It scares me, and for that reason I went very slowly, holding onto the handrail trying to step firmly, counting the steps to pass the time.

I felt a cold hand on my back and let out a scream. The old woman who'd touched me let out one herself and to top it off I had to accompany her to her door on the fourth floor. I couldn't take any more. I couldn't take care of anybody. And the old woman was grabbing my arm and pulling me down with all the weight of her body. And me, "Nine," and I waited for her to first lift her cane, then the left foot, and a little push and counted "ten" to help her; she could hardly lift her other foot. "Eleven," and her, "There's thirteen in all," and she asked me who was screaming so much a little while earlier and I answered her I didn't have any idea, I was only coming in and felt very happy because I'd just seen Ricky Martin in person. "Ay, how wonderful," she said and I replied, "Much more than that," and I left her at the door but the comment she made about the screaming kept spinning through my head, especially because I had to keep climbing up in the dark.

After the seventh floor the windows let in a little more light, letting me catch a glimpse each time there was a flash of lightening. It made things easier for me. At one moment my shadow was cast on the wall; the bottle of mineral water looked like a horn emerging from my neck. I crouched down. Rolled up in a ball next to the garbage was thrown the tissue paper Gloria used to wrap her shoe box. Angélica Durán had a handkerchief with the same design and I picked it up because I felt happy even about such a silly thing as that. A faint smell of burned rubber hung in the hallway.

When I opened the door of our apartment, I couldn't see anything. I gathered my courage and went in. I knew the place like the back of my hand. "Gloria!" I shouted in the direction of the kitchen and hallway, but no response. Very strange. "Gloria!" again; silence and then a horrible clap of thunder that made the blinds tremble. I didn't understand what could've happened for her to go out at a moment like this, with me so much to tell her and during such a storm. But she'd been behaving like a child and lately had been acting strange. Secretive and unpredictable. It seemed like the burning smell came from inside.

I let out a terrified scream, stumbling into something and almost dropping the bottle. I ran into the moving hamper and suddenly didn't know why I'd tripped. I was disorientated in the darkness and had the feeling someone had pushed me, but I always trip when there's no light.

When I was a girl I always asked my mother to leave the nightlight on because I panicked waking up in the middle of the night without anybody there. I couldn't tell where I was, couldn't remember on which side was the headboard or where my feet were. So I ended up screaming or hurt all the time.

Mama sat before the mirror in her bedroom in Gualeguaychú and drew the third line of her eye, the one almost painted on the inside to give depth. She seemed tired and older, as if the last two years weighed upon her shoulders. Even so she looked divine as always and her room smelled better than ever. She had a magazine open to the middle. Real Life Cases *with the article about the explosion. A little picture of my sister and another of me with an arrow that barely grazed the black border.*

My sister and I always fought about the same thing. She couldn't sleep with the nightlight on. And she'd get up to turn it off and then I'd shout for help, and fights, nothing but fights. Until they bought an emergency flashlight that illuminated us all night long. It was my guardian angel saving me from the dark shadows, and I would've liked to have had it with me at that moment, but it was locked in my room. I heard a slamming door from an upper floor and tripped again upon a chair. Either I was stupid or all the furniture had been moved.

Mama covered her face with transparency powder. It was her secret for looking splendid. Good make-up, she always said, is what corrects your imperfections and moreover isn't noticeable, and it was there, with the final powder, when you could verify who a true beautician was. She was wearing the most discrete one-piece black dress. She stood up and sat down again with the container of skin cream for her legs.

I really banged my knees but I didn't care. I had the strength to confront anything. I continued groping my way to the kitchen. The curtains were closed and not a speck of light entered. Then my hand touched a box of matches. I lit one and had another scare. An enormous cockroach scurried beneath the coil of a burner on the stove. I grabbed it with a ball of tissue paper, holding it an inch from my hand. "Gloria!" I shouted heading down the hallway. I thought I heard a noise nearby in the bathroom. Rain beating against the windows with the same sound a television makes when the programming is off the air.

Mama dialed Hilda De Biasio's phone number with a pen. She held it by the tip because she didn't want to smear her fingernails. "I called you ten minutes ago!" Hilda said to her worried. And mama, "I don't answer the phone because I'm scared," and the other, nothing. Silence.

I opened the refrigerator and put in the two bottles. Nélida had told me that once you begin to refrigerate certain substances, you shouldn't defrost them. It made me quite scared to think that our son was at risk inside there. I'd have to do something later to save him. Luckily I found a package of candles in the cupboard. I was getting impatient and thought it was stupid to forget about the happiness from my encounter with Ricky just because of such insignificant things as a storm or the electricity being cut.

I repeated this so I'd believe it, but I still just hated being in the dark. It was very strange not to see the pictures held up by magnets on the refrigerator door: the one from the concert on 9 de Julio Avenue, the other where Gloria and I posed with our arms around each other, but I didn't pay it much attention because my clothes were so wet I was really cold. I was so tired. Besides, the atmosphere seemed very strange. Heavy, humid. I had trouble breathing. I felt fat, and as I wasn't wearing any shoes I walked on tiptoe, scared of stepping on a cockroach.

"I'm coming over," said mama after an endless pause. Hilda hastened to say, "Bring the photo," and my mother, "Yes," so softly you almost couldn't hear her. She left the phone off the hook, turned off the light and remained a few moments in the darkness, thinking of nothing, her black dress fading into the penumbra.

With a candle on a little plate I went into the bathroom to take off my make-up. In the mirror I saw my jaw tense. "Lack of practice," I thought; I held my jawbone with two fingers and opened my mouth wide as if I were going to scream. I remembered that the furniture in the living room was all in place and told myself that the lack of light had made me lose my bearings, nothing more; it's just that in the darkness I lose my way. Everything feels out of place and I panic.

I went to put the candle on the edge of the bathtub. The first thing I saw was the ember of a cigarette glowing in the dark and exploding in the toilet. A chill seized me. Gloria was naked, standing next to the toilet with a face from beyond the grave. "You didn't hear me when I shouted for you," I said to her. "No, honey, I'm upset," she replied as she flushed the toilet, grabbing her stomach as she sat back down.

"What were you doing smoking?" I asked her, because she knew very well that I didn't like the stink of cigarettes at all. "Did I or didn't I tell you I don't feel well!" she screamed. And me, "That stinks." And her all mad, "Who are you, the FBI?" and I didn't care for that at all. I said, "Look, girl, if I'm concerned about you it's not so you'll get all bitchy." And she said she was sorry and then helped me light more candles and place them around the bathroom and all around the house, while telling me how she could sense a destructive, hypernegative energy, and she took a cigarette from atop the TV and then said, "The last one," crumpling the empty pack into a ball. Her jaw was all tense and she looked kind of pale. "You're really sick," I said trying to give her a hug, but she shrugged me off and went to look for matches in the kitchen. She was wearing the platform and so didn't drag her feet.

It had been a long time since I'd seen her naked. She had a perfect body. Well-defined hip bones. A long neck. She was a little doll. "Put on 105.5," I said. And her, "What for?" "It's a surprise," and she went to turn the radio on. I don't know if it was the candlelight or the fact she was naked, but you didn't notice her limp at all.

131

And then when I thought she was never going to stop talking about herself and body energy and blah, blah, blah without caring the least little bit how wonderful the afternoon had been for me, without worrying about Ricky's health, she asked, "What's his thing like?" right to the point, blowing smoke in my face and stubbing out the cigarette embers in the Sheraton ashtray. I thought it was a horrible question, but I had to show her with the handle of the hairbrush, and I made him look good. And when we finished with the details I took her to the kitchen, showed her the little bottle of tequila and took advantage of the moment to have a drink of water, just like that, straight from the bottle. "You have an appointment with Dr. Castillo at 9 tomorrow morning," she said. Completely apathetic. I opened the curtains so that at least the reflections from the fluorescent lights of the billboards on the street would enter.

A huge bolt of lightening split the sky; it made me a bit dizzy and I covered my ears because the noise was going to be tremendous.

Mama opened the door of the house and looked both ways. She didn't want anyone to see her. Tough luck. At that moment Benito passed by in his truck. He looked serious, with an unlit cigarette in his mouth; next to him Titina, the sales clerk from Chorus, had her hand on his leg. Benito ducked his head so mama wouldn't recognize him. Anyways she didn't realize it was him, but still waited for him to go by so she could cross the street and enter the Academy De Biasio with the magazine rolled up in her hand. Gloria's mother was sitting on the steps lighting the little altar. Mama went up to her. "I have a feeling in my chest," Hilda told her and indicated they should go up. First she lit a big candle with an image of Our Lady of Lourdes she had kept especially for mama and she froze seeing how the flame emitted sparks to every side. She threw the match down and the hiss of it going out in the plastic bucket filled with dirty water beneath the altar resounded. "Let's see," said Hilda, extending her hand, and she opened the magazine right to the page we were on.

I hurried to call Dr. Castillo's office; luckily they hadn't left yet for the day. "They're dying on me," I cried desperately, and I had to beg the secretary to give me an appointment that very evening because I didn't want them to defrost. She gave in when I mentioned Nélida Doménico, Durán, and above all the make-up artist Irma, who was like family to her.

I never suspected anything when Gloria bent down to look for something in the kitchen cupboard, but when I saw her whole body looming there I had to accept something strange was happening to her. She had her wooden platform in one hand and my Polaroid in the other. I imagined the worst. Sure enough she put the camera on the table and screamed at me, "Not one more photo!" at the same time giving it a blow that made it fly through the air in a thousand pieces. I watched the fragments bounce off the wall like an explosion. It was crazy.

I ran from the kitchen. I couldn't see anything. When I was halfway down the hallway I felt a crash near my back. Gloria had thrown the bottle of mineral water at me and I heard it bouncing an inch from my right foot. I barely had time to lock myself in my room. I felt like a cockroach, my hands were sweating, and it took me a lot of effort to bar the door and open the chest of drawers. I desperately looked for a photo of Gloria. "Esperanza Hoberól, you're finished !" she screamed from outside. "Hóberal!" I corrected her with all the force of my lungs. She was acting crazy and began to bang on the door with the platform. "Gloria De Biasio, I hate you!" I screamed at her when I saw to my surprise that she had taken down all the posters of Ricky; she hadn't even left the one stuck up with tacks on the corkboard.

I opened the closet. I didn't find anything, and she kept hitting the door with all her fury. The fucking bitch had made sure to hide all the photos and destroy my Polaroid. I had no weapons left.

Mama and Gloria's mother climbed the steps as if they were both out of it. Hilda went first, holding the candle aloft, and once at the top she took mama by the hand and sat her down across the table. "What time is it?" she asked. "I don't know," mama said, trying to bring her watch close to the flame. And Gloria's mother, "Look!" and the candle was all sky blue like it never naturally appears, and the flame grew and split again into barely delineated orange and lilac and then again sky blue and on and on.

I was so ravaged and afflicted in my room I couldn't think. To one side on the floor Gloria's shoe box and inside it the little body of my dark-skinned Barbie Jocelyn all beat up, with nine other little feet burned and tortured with cigarettes, their edges melted and chewed up. I couldn't believe it. The smell of burned rubber came from there, from Gloria's *secrétaire*, and in one corner was my fan club membership card ripped in half and I could picture her moving her hands like a weasel. The only thing in it were pictures of me, pierced with a safety pin. My stomach turned. I was falling apart.

A loud noise and the door flew open with a blow. She came limping in directly to where I was bent over and gave me a whack with her platform on the right leg that almost knocked me out. I still managed to trip her and escape. She had hit me with all she could right in the bone and the pain was so intense that I only managed to get away by crawling on all fours. Broken glass covered the floor but I didn't care. She followed me with the tenacity of a mad woman, repeating, "I'm going to cleanse you," with her wooden platform shoe held high and her tits hanging loose.

I must have gone into some kind of emotional coma because I couldn't think. My movements seemed robotic, as if I'd lost all feeling. Frozen and with my back to her, with a general feeling of nausea, trying to open the kitchen window, seeing how my hand turned in slow motion, hearing my own desperate scream, and Ricky opening his arms to me from off-stage and the lights from the street flowed down with the rain and then the dry blow fell on the back of my neck and see how my nose smashes into the glass and my right hand, too, with my thumb up, like when Gloria and I saluted each other on the stage in Gualeguaychú, but this time she was behind me. It took an instant.

In the window's reflection was the flame from three candles and in the center Ramón singing in the Church of Christ and upon him the green spotlight that brought out the angles in his face and the enormous sign with twinkling lights at the back of the Church of the Eucharist of Prayer. "The glory of God will embrace our hope," I was reading when she finished me off with three more blows to the head. "Killer, devil, crazy!" she screamed while beating me, and the neon signs in the streets twinkling.

Then, with absolute calm, she got dressed, put on her platform, grabbed the bottle of semen in the refrigerator and before leaving threw out the box with my photos and the little doll feet. She passed an egg over my entire body and then smashed it on my right leg.

When she slammed the door I heard my own voice on the radio. The message I'd left a little earlier on 105.5 began, where I asked Ricky to forgive me, I asked mama why she never came to look for me, and I asked Gloria for help. I said I loved her with all my heart and recently she had been like the sister I never had, I was dedicating to her Ricky's latest, "You'll Be Back"; you could tell from my voice I was crying with emotion and you could hear the wooden platform banging on the steps of my home, going off in the distance with a *toc* that finally blended into the song beginning on the radio.

Three minutes later, before Ricky had finished the song, I stopped breathing.

Gloria got me ready with the elaboration that the people from Salta fix up their *equecos* for Carnaval. She wrapped me up in an ordinary bedspread and put all my belongings into little nylon bags. In one the remains of the bottle of mineral water and another the destroyed Polaroid. The picture of Nélida Doménico with me in her arms, Irma's fake braid, the poster of Ricky half-naked, the little doll feet in their cardboard box, my embroidered handkerchief and my photo albums of Ricky with the autographs of Menudo. She tied me up with the fifteen feet or so of the banner that

I'd hung on the wall saying, "I love you" with my name written in red and yellow letters and then she put me in the moving hamper.

She cleaned up everything and when the masseur arrived from Devoto she was ready and had her make-up on. Gloria hugged him while he took a piss and they passed the time until 3:30 a.m.

They pushed the hamper down the hallway and dragged it down nine floors, step by step, and finally put me in the back of his truck.

The fat guy tuned in the weather forecast. Isolated showers were expected any time but the storm had let up. At a stoplight they sat a bit listening to the first descriptions of Princess Di's funeral, broadcast live from London, the casket drawn by two horses, a divine red and yellow altar cloth draped over it completely, and thousands of flowers.

There wasn't a soul on the street. They had the whole city to themselves, so they pulled over and waited a lot but always ended up convinced it was better to keep going. We finally stopped about a hundred yards from the Fishermen's Club, where a sign with a white arrow pointed to the sky. They dragged me along again between them and threw me from a place where there wasn't any railing.

It all happened quickly and I immediately sank from the weight of my memories and the manhole cover they had tied to my head; I went straight down and stuck in the river bottom. And Gloria, on the bank, in her turquoise blouse with red pompoms, watching how I disappeared into the water, with all the muscles of her face tensed and a horrible wind blowing that kept messing up her hair. In Gualeguaychú the candle between Hilda De Biasio and mama went out at the moment I went under.

When mama went to light it again, Gloria's mother had already extended her hand at the height of her forehead and lowered it down to her chin.

And perhaps my story might have been just another case from "People Searching for People." And Gloria would have been left with all the glory. But she didn't know or didn't remember that we Hóberals or Hoberóls (however the hell she says it) come back to speak, even when we're dead.

Mass Media Totalitarianism: Hope Over All
an afterword by Daniel Link

It's difficult to present a first novel, especially when the work, like *Die, Lady, Die,* is destined from the outset to raze like a storm our preconceived notions about literature. And I don't refer here to the absolutely eccentric little world of Argentine literature, but to contemporary writing, what's called "world literature": *Die, Lady, Die* claims its place among current novels, independent of any language or nationality, precisely because it speaks of something with neither language nor nationality: pop culture, the industrial culture out of which we are now accustomed to mold our desires and our fears.

The plot is simple and the story develops like an arrow shot straight forward: an adolescent girl from the provinces (thrown out of a dysfunctional family) travels to the big city. The point of departure is Gualeguaychú, in Entre Ríos, Argentina, and the point of destination is Buenos Aires, but it's the same as if we had imagined Los Angeles and Springfield, a town where there is only one of everything. One record store, one school, one radio station, one discotheque, one boyfriend, one lover and one sole desire: to escape from a stifling, monotonous life, conquer the big city and accomplish a dream that not repeated, mass produced and made vulgar loses its power to disconnect from the awareness of its own past, its own terrors and the truth of its own body, all of which *Die, Lady, Die* sets forth with a force unusual in most contemporary narrative.

The protagonist and narrator of this story is named Esperanza (Hope) Hóberal (over all, or if you prefer, all over). Hope everywhere. Hope above all/everyone? Hope is all over. What the novel attempts to explain is that passage, that transformation, in any case that question of and about Hope.

Esperanza (Hope) leaves Gualeguaychú (Springfield) with one sole desire (hope): to have a baby with Ricky Martin. When the pop idol, whom the young woman had earlier met when the former member of Menudo was just starting out as a soloist, mocks her by saying he wants to have a baby with Lady Di, she knows that she must eliminate the princess (who, more than once, appears as her doppelgänger). The death of Princess Di, in the framework between paranoid and schizophrenic that *Die, Lady, Die* proposes, is a result of the desire (hope), the desperation and the enchantment that Esperanza (Hope) utilizes to finish off her enemy.

Not that Esperanza hopes and waits for glory (for which she first would need a plan); rather, she always believes that glory (her friend Gloria) awaits her. Fatally, Esperanza is wrong and dies. The novel's last sentence (which could well come from the film *Sunset Boulevard*, that wonderful Billy Wilder melodrama about glory where the dead also speak), carries hope/Hope beyond death and there in that beyond everything will, perhaps, be laid out.

Alejandro López's novel *Die, Lady, Die* is contemporaneous with *Mulholland Drive* (2001), a film that shares completely its spirit and undertaking (although not style, which in the case of the Argentine is much lighter, much more irreverent): Lynch's film also concerns a young woman who goes on a journey supposing that glory somewhere awaits her and as well, fatally, the young woman runs into death. As in López's novel, there are hallucinations, moments of sorcery, and passions of the body and soul impossible to satisfy.

Perhaps for such reasons critics in Argentina and Brazil (where the novel has also been translated) have insisted on associating *Die, Lady, Die* with a certain modern "Bovarism." Like Emma Bovary, Esperanza is frivolous because she is hostage to other people's conventions: Latino kitsch, lonely hearts magazines, *TV Guide*, the frightful imagination of teenage culture that television and pop music diffuse. But it is that maniacal imagination (which makes many people, including Ricky Martin, scream at her, "You're crazy!") that turns Esperanza, like Emma, into a tragic figure.

This last comment isn't made capriciously. The author has been sure to emphasize the point during interviews. And there it is for any attentive reader in Chapter 7, where an erotic sequence is superimposed upon a religious service, exactly as in the famous chapter in Flaubert's novel. One needn't dwell on López's preoccupation for pointing out family resemblance as a trait of gravity or temerity (compare this with Flaubert). Rather here is a declaration of love: love for literature but also love for his character. That Flaubert condemns his heroine to such a terrible death is key to understanding that immeasurable, and rather out-of-place, love. In *Flaubert's Parrot* (a novel that López surely read with all our same passion), Julian Barnes gives testimony of this mad love that has, since the beginning of our modern times, dangerously but inevitably mixed with the imagination (the imagination of pop culture: the imagination of our era).

Die, Lady, Die can't be understoond only as satire (although it's a ferocious satire in the same way as *Madame Bovary*) without betraying all that López's novel draws upon from Flaubert: even the most frivolous and most provincial character is a heroine and, as such, the possible object of an *amour fou*. It's in this tragic dimension that the novel resides.

Might one consider the author a more popular Cortázar? Perhaps what interests López (born in Goya, Corrientes in 1968, and a finalist with *Die, Lady, Die* for the 1999 Premio Clarín) is showing the darkest part of daily life and the way in which the most domestic begins to give form to the monstrous. Esperanza is a monster, as are almost all the other characters in *Die, Lady, Die*, including celebrities.

In fact, one could say of this novel the same thing the great poet Arturo Carrera said of contemporary Argentine poetry, which shares with *Die, Lady, Die* more than one characteristic: "'A great part of contemporary poetry and art—perhaps the most representative—is characterized by its particular perception of the monstrous as a daily fact, as an alienated world, as habit.' And if indeed it's certain that some poets seem to fit this category perfectly, Leónidas Lamborghini's thesis holds up by pointing out a distinctive trait common to all the poets of the '80s and '90s: the constant intersection of theories of daily perception where the humorous, the grotesque, the ironically lyrical, the absurdity common to horror and laughter, assimilate all distortion and return it reproduced over and over: an approach to 'absolutely dispassionate' language no longer indifferent to the tension of language. The poetry of young writers seems to focus for us more closely on the trivial nature of talk, indeed including talk made tense as if by some classical realism; except that in such a forced reality we again encounter the supernatural nature of poetry and its way of activating that reality..."

The monster, Alejandro López surely knows, represents a threat to the system of reproduction and lineage, and so staggers upon the lettered scaffolding, the scene of writing. And thus it's constantly necessary to catch, capture, stalk it. The monster imagines a festival but encounters a hunt in which itself (and only itself) is the victim: hope is all over. And so let us reject hurried classifications (also trap-like tools): López related to Manuel Puig and Copi? Perhaps, but not *certainly*. (With respect to Puig, López has said, "All we have in common is that we're both from a small town.") In any case, closer to Flaubert's *amour fou* than anything else.

Definitely, as the Argentine writer Fogwill has pointed out, "To think of *Die, Lady, Die* in a literary salon twenty or twenty-five years ago is the best way to understand its novelty and freshness. One might also draw comparisons with the '20s and Borges, and his obstinate rewriting in search of a tone of voice, and the Borgesian certainty that everything resides in the tone: what's important, the events, their verisimilitude and the plot, the pleasure of the reader." Take pleasure here, reader, before Esperanza (that is, Hope) dies.

Daniel Link, a 2004 Guggenheim Fellow, teaches twentieth-century literature at the Universidad de Buenos Aires.

His publications include the novels *Los años noventa* and *La ansiedad*; the poetry collection *La clausura de febrero y otros poemas malos*; and the collections of essays *La chancha con cadenas*, *Cómo se lee*, and *El juego de los cautos*. Link has also edited the work of the Argentine writer Rodolfo Walsh (*El violento oficio de escribir* and *Ese hombre y otros papeles personales*).
www.linkillo.blogspot.com

Translator's Acknowledgements

Thanks to the Fundación Teoría y Práctica de las Artes (TyPA) in Buenos Aires, Argentina, for facilitating contact with Adriana Hidalgo editora; a special thanks to Gabriela Adamo at TyPA for her personal interest, effort and ongoing support.

Daniel Link of the Universidad de Buenos Aires was generous enough to introduce Alejandro López and his work to the English-speaking audience.

Walter Pitt of Salvation in Minneapolis came up with the killer title.

As always, Jason the Argonaut and *la flaca* give me reason for everything I do.

JM, San Pablo Etla, Oaxaca

January 2005